Lark Rise to Candleford

Two plays

Keith Dewhurst
from Flora Thompson's trilogy

Samuel French — London
New York - Toronto - Hollywood

Please see page iv for further copyright information

CONTENTS

COPYRIGHT INFORMATION

(See also page ii)

INTRODUCTION:
THE PROMENADE PLAY

Lark Rise and *Candleford* were written to be performed as promenade productions. That is to say, there was no distinction between stage and auditorium; the seats were taken out, the audience was free to walk around and the actors performed the play in the middle of them. Sometimes the actors could not even see the colleagues to whom they were speaking because there were too many spectators in between. This is obviously opposed to that conventional notion of theatre in which the audience sits more or less comfortably in rows and the curtain rises to reveal a picture of life from which the 'fourth wall' has been removed.

In fact that type of conventional theatre, like its great masters Ibsen and Chekhov, was the creation of the nineteenth century and of sophisticated electrical and scenic devices that for the first time in the two-and-a-half thousand year history of drama produced a convincing imitation of 'real' appearances. The proscenium arch divided the space occupied by the actors from that occupied by the audience, and both actors and playwrights had to behave as though the audience did not exist.

If the play was 'real', writers could not use dramatic tricks that were 'unreal', such as the Elizabethan soliloquy, the asides of classical comedy, and a device like the Greek chorus, which speaks a running commentary directly to the audience. For the same reason, traditionally powerful effects like music and dance were rarely seen in a straight play, and the notion behind a work like Shakespeare's *Henry IV*, where the action moves swiftly from place to place and from one social class to another, so that the theatre can display an entire society, became almost impossible to realize in modern conditions: it was too expensive and the scenes took too long to change.

Plays were set in dining-rooms and studies, or an atmospherically lit garden, and presented great themes through everyday events. The spectacular, and thus the more popular broad-based, aspects of theatre were still seen in musicals and pantomime, but hardly at all in the modern 'serious' theatre, except for classical revivals. Yet the English dramatic tradition, from medieval mystery plays to Shakespeare and Victorian melodramas, is essentially epic and popular; it is rough and tumble, or else it would not have survived so long, and that is why its spectacular elements were bound to burst out again sooner or later.

At the same time we must not forget what a great deal was gained by the new drama of the nineteenth century: for authors, a sense of structure and the very possibility of a steady 'serious' public; for actors, a coherent discipline, best expressed by Stanislavski, that enabled them to present what they knew to be artificial in a way that related to our notions of what is rational and realistic. Another legacy was bricks and mortar: hundreds of theatres, all over the world, many with marvellous gilt and plush, all valuable real-estate and all with proscenium arches.

And then along came cinema, with its seemingly absolute and overwhelming realism; and then television, which brought the cowboys and Indians into your living-room. So is it surprising that one of the most interesting developments in the contemporary theatre has been the uncoordinated but very definite striving of many people in many countries to break down the proscenium arch and make audience and actors share the same space and the same thrilling event?

As long ago as 1929, the director Tyrone Guthrie had steps built down from the stage to the stalls of the Arts Theatre, Cambridge, and twenty years later he saw his ideas realized in a literally concrete form when at his insistence the Shakespeare Theatre at Stratford, Ontario, was built as a theatre-in-the-round so it could present plays written in widely different conventions. What has happened in England since then is the subsidy-assisted boom of the 1950s and 1960s, which among other things enabled English writers to write epic plays again, and also financed dozens of new theatres, many of them with multi-purpose stages. Joan Littlewood made her great statements on the notion of a popular theatre, and in scores of fringe and studio theatres actors and audiences learned to confront each other at close range again. The theatre today is exciting precisely because many different of kinds of work exist side-by-side, and it is more than likely that if Bill Bryden and I had not done a production like *Lark Rise*, someone else would.

At the same time it marked a definite stage in work that as a writer-director partnership we have developed over a number of years: epic plays with music that have gradually evolved into a promenade style. If this style has other, conscious points of reference I would say that they are *Orlando Furioso*, the famous arena-style production by Ronconi which Bill saw at the Edinburgh Festival; *1789*, which I saw at the Cartoucherie de Vincennes in April 1971, and William Gaskill's *The Speakers*, a promenade production which we both saw, and about which I wrote an article in the *Guardian* in 1974. It was also William Gaskill who brought Bill Bryden and me together, in December 1970, to do an epic play called *Pirates*, in a Royal Court Sunday night performance without décor.

It is worth noting that three actors in *Pirates*, Jack Shepherd, Derek Newark and Brian Glover, appeared at one time or another in *Lark Rise*, and that members of the folk-rock group, Steeleye Span, played in both the play and the foyer.

In January 1971 we did a show in which we transformed the Theatre Upstairs into an army canteen with a boxing ring, for a performance of Brecht's *The Baby Elephant*, to which I added a cabaret-prologue about Brecht himself. The cast included three more actors, Dave Hill, Bob Hoskins and Mark McManus, who have appeared in Cottesloe plays; so the hard core of a company was formed a long time ago. In May 1971 we did *Corunna!*, a Napoleonic Wars ballad-opera for five actors and five musicians of Steeleye Span, among them Maddy Prior, who was in two Cottesloe plays, and Martin Carthy, who was in *Lark Rise*.

Corunna! was played on a central ramp with the audience in rows on each side, an arrangement that we repeated at the Cottesloe Theatre in November 1978 for *The World Turned Upside Down*. After a week at the Theatre Upstairs, *Corunna!* toured the kind of one-night-stand rock dates at which the band then appeared: from university unions to the concert room of the St George's Hall in Liverpool and a proscenium theatre in Harrogate.

Bill Bryden subsequently moved to the Royal Lyceum Theatre, Edinburgh, where in 1972 we did an adaptation with the regrouped Steeleye Span of R. L. Stevenson's *Kidnapped*, and although we played the climax of the play like a concert, with the actors facing out front on a row of chairs, I think we both felt that the proscenium arch was not really suited to that kind of work; our other joint show there, in 1973, was an orthodox version of Molière's *The Miser*. In 1974 I wrote a play with music for the Birmingham Repertory Theatre, and in 1977 Bill became the artistic director of the Cottesloe Theatre, the National Theatre's smallest auditorium, which in fact has a capacity of over 400 and is a multi-purpose space stunningly designed by Iain Mackintosh.

At Easter 1977 Bill, with his associate Sebastian Graham-Jones, was able to realize for one week in the Cottesloe a long-cherished project of excerpts, entitled *The Passion*, from the medieval English mystery plays. These were adapted by the poet Tony Harrison and had music by the Albion Band, whose leader Ashley Hutchings had played with Steeleye Span in *Corunna! The Passion* was done in full promenade style, and as a result of its success I was commissioned to adapt *Lark Rise* for performance in March 1978.

For some time we had discussed using books as the basis of plays, because a lot of our work, and crucially much of the fine integration of music and action, is done in rehearsal, so the basic property — as well as the trust of all the people in each other — needs to be very solid. Also, books bring an audience with them, and we have always reached for what is epic and popular, and used music and spectacle because when there is a band in the space the event takes on vital aspects of a concert: the immediacy and the ability to speak directly to the audience.

If one can generalize about the actors in what the press have called the "Cottesloe company", it is to say that they have been chosen because they are high-energy character-players, strongly centred in their own accents, regions and experiences of life; and in the promenade their energy is more closely experienced than in any other kind of theatre.

The overall aim of the productions is to entertain without loss of seriousness or of high standards of text, acting and music: to create an experience that will appeal on different levels to as many people as possible. *Lark Rise to Candleford* is clearly ideal material for such an event. Flora Thompson was a writer of sharp honesty who described the epic transition from the ancient agrarian life to the modern world in simple everyday terms.

The only problem was that *Lark Rise* is a book without a narrative, whose chapters each describe a different aspect of life in the hamlet in which Flora grew up. The solution to this was to make the action of the play the events of a single day — the first day of harvest because that seemed the most typical — and to attach dialogue and scenes from all parts of the book to that thread. The music was a natural province of the Albion Band, and the flash forward to the Great War was obvious when one visited Cottisford Church and saw the memorial tablet mentioned at the end of the book. This visit also gave the designer, William Dudley, the idea for his magnificent set, for at Juniper Hill where Flora lived the impression of flat fields and sky is overwhelming, and this could be simulated in the design of the skycloth, wheat field and cottage. The part of the play that had to be most carefully written without betraying the spirit of the book was the sadness of the relationship between Flora's father and mother.

When we came to *Candleford* it seemed natural to contrast a day in summer with a day in winter. There is more narrative in the last book of Flora Thompson's trilogy; she combined two villages into one "Candleford Green", and the play concentrates on events which took place at one of them, Fringford in Oxfordshire, where Flora worked in the post office-cum-blacksmith's run by Mrs Whitton, fictionalized as Dorcas Lane. This play ends with a flash forward to Flora's own unhappy married life, a scene that I did not write in its present form until the preview before opening night.

When read, these plays seem more like film or television scripts than ordinary plays. That is because the promenade enables one to cut away and, if the actors pull focus strongly, to achieve very brief effects indeed. The plays are more subtly promenade than *The Speakers*, where the setting was Hyde Park, or *The Passion*, where it was the streets. In those plays the audience exist in the same time and place as the actors, but in *Lark Rise* the actors are in 1880 and the audience in the present, and this calls for true concentration: there is a great and gentle skill in making a person who does not exist move out of your way!

No doubt the plays would work in other arenas, but in the promenade the experience of each member of the audience is his or hers alone. No-one sees all the play, although if it can be heard it can be followed, and some emotions must be read off the faces of other spectators. In a way each person is his or her own television camera, and at the same time part of the show. The audience and the actors create together an event that is a celebration of Flora Thompson. She was unique, a great writer, and what is celebrated is the common humanity that she shared with us, and with the Oxfordshire villagers, long dead.

KEITH DEWHURST 1980

Lark Rise was first performed in 1978 and I wrote this introduction for the original published edition of the plays in 1980. Because it still seems a very fair account of how the plays came to be written I have let it stand: my only regret is that apart from a lunchtime piece for the students of the Western Australian Academy of Performing Arts in 1984, I have not had the opportunity to develop further the idea of promenade theatre.

KEITH DEWHURST 1995

MUSIC

In many cases specific dramatic effects were conceived with specific tunes in mind, e.g. the Battle of the Somme at the end of *Lark Rise*, and the plays will work much better if the original tunes are used.

Copies of all the music for *Lark Rise* and of music written for *Candleford* is available on hire from Samuel French Ltd. Other music for *Candleford* may be found in found in folk music libraries and hymn books.

LARK RISE

CHARACTERS

Laura, 10
Edmund, 8
Emma Timms, Laura and Edmund's mother
Albert Timms, Laura and Edmund's father

Farm labourers:
Bishie, Bill Miller
Boamer, Dick Tuffrey
Pumpkin, Tom Gaskin
Old Price
Old David, David's father

Mr Morris, Bailiff — "Old Monday Morning"

Fisher, youth
Stut

Mrs Spicer, leader of the women's gang
Mrs Blaby
Mrs Peverill
Mrs Miller
Old Sally, 80
Dick, her husband
Old Postie, the postman
Mr Sharman, the Major
Doctor
Carrier
Grandfather, Emma's father
Queenie Macey
Twister, her husband, gamekeeper
Jerry Parish, fish/fruit cart
Martha Beamish, 12
Mrs Beamish
Squire Bracewell
John Price, son of Old Price
Mrs Andrews
Garibaldi Jacket

Cheapjack
Tramp
Polly, John Price's girl
Landlord of pub
Algy
Mr Pridham, band singer
Rector
Sam
Cockie
Chad Gubbins

SYNOPSIS OF SCENES

LARK RISE

Commissioned by the National Theatre and first presented at the Cottesloe
Theatre on 29th March 1978, with the following cast:

Old Price, Dick, Grandfather	John Barrett
Mr Pridham, Sam, singer	Martin Carthy
Boamer, Cheapjack	Warren Clarke
Singer	Shirley Collins
Mrs Peverill, Queenie Macey	Edna Dore
Laura	Caroline Embling
Mr Morris, Jerry Parish, Landlord	Brian Glover
Stut, Twister, Algy, Tramp	Howard Goorney
Old David, Major Sharman, Rector	Michael Gough
Fisher, John Price, Carrier	Glyn Grain
Albert Timms	James Grant
Edmund	Laurence Hardiman
Martha Beamish, Polly	Louisa Livingstone
Emma Timms	Mary Miller
Pumpkin, Doctor, Squire Bracewell	Derek Newark
Bishie, Postie	Trevor Ray
Mrs Blaby, Mrs Beamish, Garibaldi Jacket	Dinah Stubb
Cockie, singer	John Tams
Mrs Spicer, Old Sally, Mrs Miller, Mrs Andrews	June Watson

Directed by Bill Bryden and Sebastian Graham-Jones
Designed by William Dudley
Musical Director, Ashley Hutchings
Music by the Albion Band

LARK RISE

*The band welcomes the audience into the space with a tune. When the Lights
go down the actors form up in a photo pose, and as the Lights come up again,
the band singers begin "Arise and Pick a Posy"*

Song

Band   Hark says the fair maid
The nightingales are singing
The larks are winging
Their notes up in the air.
Small birds and turtle doves
On every bough are building,
The sun is just a glimmering
Arise my dear.

Rise up my fair one
And pick your love a posy
It is the finest flower
That ever my eyes did see.
Yes I will pick you posies,
Sweet lily pink and rosy;
There is none so fair a flower
As the lad I adore.

Lennady, Lennady
You are a lovely creature,
You are the finest flower
That ever my eyes did see.

I play you a tune
All on the pipes of ivory,
So early in the morning
Before break of day.

Arise and pick a posy,
Sweet lily, pink and rosy;

It is the finest flower
That ever I did see.
Small birds and turtle doves
On every bough are building,
The sun is just a glimmering
Arise my dear.

*The cast has now dispersed except for Laura, who is a small skinny girl of 10
with dark eyes and pale yellow hair*

Laura (*to the audience*) The hamlet stood on a gentle rise in the flat, wheat-growing north-east corner of Oxfordshire. We will call it Lark Rise because of the great number of skylarks which made the surrounding fields their springboard and nested on the bare earth between the rows of green corn. For a few days or a week or a fortnight, the fields stood "ripe unto harvest". It was the one perfect period in the hamlet year. The 1880s brought a succession of hot summers, and day after day, as harvest time approached, the children of the end house would wake to the dewy pearly pink of a fine summer dawn, and the swizzh, swizzh of the early morning breeze rustling through the ripe corn beyond their doorstep ...

*Laura's brother Edmund appears, yawning and rubbing his eyes. He is 8
years old, and tall for his age, with blue eyes and regular features*

Oh, come on, Edmund. Come you on.
Edmund What are we goin' for?
Laura Mushrooms, Edmund.
Edmund (*excited*) Mushrooms?!
Laura Sssh! Mushrooms!

*Laura and Edmund lose themselves in the wheat-field that is the audience.
The light is the pearly pink of dawn*

ACT I

SCENE 1

It is morning. In the end house, Laura's father, Albert Timms, is eating a piece of bread and lard. He is a slim, upright man with fiery eyes and raven-black hair. He wears strong, light-grey worsted clothes because his work is dusty. He is a stonemason and walks three miles to his employers in the market town. He dislikes living in the hamlet and considers himself better than his neighbours

Albert looks round for his dinner basket but can't see it. He calls upstage to his wife Emma

Albert Emmie! Emmie!
Emma Sssh ... !
Albert Where's my dinner basket?
Emma You'll wake up Laura and Edmund.
Albert Oh, they be up and gone out, woman.

Emma comes downstairs. She is graceful and her copper-coloured hair hangs loose. She was once a nursemaid in a good family

Emma Gone out? Where? Are they after mushrooms again?
Albert Ay.
Emma Those fields are soaked with dew.
Albert Ay.
Emma Six-shillingsworth of good shoe-leather gone for six-pennorth of mushrooms!
Albert He's quick as a flash our Edmund.
Emma Course he is.
Albert We must apprentice him to a good trade. Carpenters, perhaps. A man with a good trade's *sure* of his living.
Emma (*giving him the packed dinner basket she has found*) You won't stay late tonight, will you? Not again?
Albert Stay late? With the likes of you waiting?

He kisses her. Their mutual attraction is strong

What was it that gentleman called you when you worked at the big house? Pocket Venus, wasn't it?

Emma Quite nicely, Albert. He was married with no nonsense about him.

They smile and kiss again

Albert I think we'll give notice on this place, eh? Move over to Candleford.
Emma Ay.
Albert When the old pig's killed I'll give notice.
Emma Ay.
Albert Can't never move with an old pig, can we?
Emma No.

He is ready. He picks up his dinner basket, his apron and tools, and slaps on his billycock hat

Albert How do I look, eh? Like a proper stonemason, eh?
Emma You won't stop late, Albert.
Albert I told you, woman.

Emma is upset by his burst of temper and grievance but determined not to part badly

Emma Now let's not part bad. Let's not make it like Dick's hatband, that went half-way round and tucked.

Albert also wants to part well. He sighs and gently kisses her

Albert You go back up, Emma, and have your beauty sleep.

Albert steps outside the house. All over the hamlet men are coming out of their cottages. They are farm labourers. The young men have drooping walrus moustaches, the elders a fringe of grey whisker beneath the jaw, extending from ear to ear. One or two old men still have smocks and round black felt hats but most wear corduroy trousers and an unbleached drill jacket called a "Slopps". Some have rush-plaited hats and some billycocks

Bill Miller (nicknamed "Bishie") meets Dick Tuffrey (nicknamed "Boamer") and his father Old David Tuffrey

Bishie Morning, Boamer. Morning, Master Tuffrey.
Boamer Morning, Bishie.
Old David Morning, young Bill.

Tom Gaskin, nicknamed Pumpkin, comes out of his cottage

Boamer Morning, Pumpkin.
Pumpkin Morning, lads.
Bishie Think weather's a-gooin' to hold?
Pumpkin Till us get 'un all in?
Bishie Ay.
Pumpkin Ay.
Old David Course it's a-gooin' to hold.

Albert walks in the opposite direction, towards the town. He would pass the men without speaking and they know it. They nudge each other and point

Bishie Look 'ee who's here.
Boamer Think he'll not speak nor nothin'?
Bishie No. Not him.

Albert walks past them without speaking

Pumpkin *(calling after him)* Morning, Mr Timms.
Albert *(stopping and turning)* Tom Gaskin?
Pumpkin Ay.
Albert Morning. Morning all.
Old David Morning.
Albert Morning.

He manages a nod and a smile for Old David. Then he strides off

Bishie Now let me ask you, Master Tuffrey — did you ever, in all your draggin'-up, see a man so stinking with pride?
Boamer Bricklayer calling himself a stonemason.
Old David Say what us will, I respect his missus.
Pumpkin Ay. Oh ay. But all the same she says his family kept an hotel in Oxford: but my wife's cousin knowed fer a fac' it weren't more nor a pot-house.

The men laugh. Old Price appears from his house

Old Price Morning, David.
Old David Morning.
Old Price Morning, boys.
Boamer Morning, Master Price. Think weather's a-gooin' to hold?
Old Price Till we get 'un in? Course it's a-gooin' to hold.
Pumpkin It'll hold fer you, Master Price, what's seen a few harvests in your time.

Old Price I have, Pumpkin: and I hope I'll see a girt lot more.

They all laugh

Bishie Look us all here now. Bailiff's a-waitin'.

Other men are congregating in the yard of the manor farm. The bailiff, Mr Morris, is a tall, shrivelled, nutcracker-faced old fellow swishing an ash stick. The men call him "Old Monday Morning"

Morris Hi men! Ho men! Monday morning. What do you reckon you're doing?
Pumpkin They're all a-coomin' up, Muster Morris!
Voices Morning, Sam. Morning, Cockie.
Morris Monday morning. Hi men! Ho men! Be ye deaf, or be ye hard of hearing, dang ye? Hurry up, men!
Bishie Hark at Old Monday Morning!
Morris Hi men! Ho! Call this harvest morning? Today's Monday, tomorrow's Tuesday, next day's Wednesday — half the week gone and nothing done!
Fisher Us've harnessed every team up, Muster Morris!

As Morris turns his back to look at Fisher, Boamer points at him with one hand and with the other slaps his own buttocks

Boamer My elbow to you, you old devil!
Morris What's that? What's that?
Boamer Just a-asking this little gallass what's the matter, Muster Morris.

The gallass is a youth nicknamed Fisher

Fisher Got my boots wet, Boamer — now 'um dried as stiff as boards.
Old Price Boots? Good thing you didn't live when breeches were made o'leather.
Bishie Have patience. Remember Job.

Laughter

Fisher Job? What did he know 'bout patience? He didn't have to wear no leather breeches.

His quickness draws a mildly jeering response. Then a latecomer arrives

Pumpkin Here's old Stut late for his own funeral ... Morning, Stut.

Old Stut M-M-Morning, P-P-Pumpkin.

Morris Hi men! Ho men! Now men! We'll put the mechanical reaper in Gibbard's Piece. Will your boots stop you driving the team, young Fisher?

Muttered voices

Bishie He's young Job!

Pumpkin Wooman's work!

Boamer Well, he's nothin' nor a boychap!

Fisher I'll see what I can do, Muster Morris, sir.

Morris I'll send the women's gang to bind up after you. Mrs Spicer? Ho! Mrs Spicer!

Mrs Spicer Here I be, Muster Morris! (*The leader of the women's gang, she is formidable in a pair of her husband's corduroy trousers*)

Morris Hi there! Ho there! What?

Old Price Speak up, Mrs Spicer.

Mrs Spicer Eh?

Fisher Monday Morning can't hear you.

Old Price You're as hoarse as a crow.

Pumpkin As ugly as sin, more like.

Mrs Spicer You rub your mouth with salt, young Pumpkin!

The men thoroughly appreciate this exchange

Morris Gibbard's Piece, Mrs Spicer! Gibbard's Piece! Now men. Hi men! We'll set to with the scythes in Hundred Acre Field. What d'you think of that?

Bishie Set us more than us can do and us'll do it!

Pumpkin You'll not never need them jibberin' old Irish gypsies this year, Muster Morris!

Morris Farmer and his wife have provided some good ale as usual and I'll be riding round with it! I'll be riding, men! Have you chosen your King of the Mowers?

All Ay! We have that! Ay!

Morris Who is it?

Bishie Boamer!

Cheers and a bit of backslapping

Old Price Wert up, Boamer lad!

Boamer Thank God for having growed the corn up right, Muster Morris, for us'll bring 'un down all right, eh, boys?

All That us will! Good old Boamer!

Morris You lead the line, Boamer. You say when they rest. You say what
  drinks they take. Monday morning! Ho there! Hi there!
Old Price Come on, Boamer, lad. On with your hat, then!

*They put Boamer's flowered hat on him and then lift him on to their shoulders.
He is then handed a sickle and repeats the ritual rhyme*

Rhyme

> I have lawns, I have bowers
> I have fruit, I have flowers
> And the lark be my morning alarmer.
>
> To the parson his tithe
> Here's good luck to the scythe
> Success and long life to the farmer

*Cheering, the men carry Boamer to the field, where they let him down and
form up in a line with their scythes*

Boamer Follow me, lads, for I'm your King of the Mowers!

*Then they mow the wheat field in line to the accompaniment of the "Harvest
Work Song"*

Song

Men   When harvest come on and the reaping begins,
                      The farmer the fruit of the earth gathers in.
                      In mirth let us talk till the season be gone,
                      And at night give a holler till it's all of a row, till it's all of
                        a row,
                      And at night give a holler till it's all of a row.

                      Then early next morning our hooks we do grind,
                      And away to the cornfields to reap and to bind.
                      Our foreman looks back and he leaves well behind,
                      And he gives a loud holler, bring it all well behind, bring it
                        all well behind,
                      And he gives a loud holler, bring it all well behind.

                      O then says the foreman, behind and before,
                      We will have a fresh whet and half a pint more.

So me jolly boys to the end we will go,
To the end we will go till it's all of a row, till it's all of a row,
To the end we will go till it's all of a row.

When night it comes on to the farm we will steer,
To partake a good supper and to drink a strong beer.
In wishing the farmer such blessings in his life,
And in drinking a health unto him and his wife, unto him
and his wife,
And in drinking a health unto him and his wife.

Our wheat is all in, oats, barley are bound,
Here's success to the farmer who ploughs through the
ground,
As for this wheat stubble into turnips we'll sow,
And so we'll continue till it's all of a row, till it's all of a row,
And so we'll continue till it's all of a row.

Last refrain repeated as necessary

SCENE 2

*Laura and Edmund have returned to the end house and both they and their
mother are enjoying the fried mushrooms. Emma is dressed now and her hair
is parted in the middle and drawn down to a knot at the back. The children
do not speak while eating*

Emma Edmund. Sit up, Edmund!

Edmund sits up

Six-shillingsworth of good shoe-leather gone for six-pennorth of mushrooms!

Laura opens her mouth

Little girls should be seen and not heard.

*Laura does not speak. She returns to her mushrooms. She finishes and looks
at Edmund. He is still eating. Then Edmund finishes. Their mother looks at
them*

Now what d'you do?

Laura folds her hands to say grace. Edmund follows suit

Laura Thank God for my good breakfast. Thank Father and Mother. Amen.
Edmund Amen.
Emma Amen.
Laura I didn't wear no boots and gave Edmund my old ones.
Emma Going out without boots? You must be cold as ice.

Silence. Laura and Mother have not quite made it up

Edmund Mother.
Emma What.
Edmund What's the sea like?
Emma It's big, Edmund. Now don't go asking me questions.

Mother starts to clear the table. Laura helps her

Edmund Is it as big as Cottesloe Pond?
Emma Good Lord, yes.
Edmund How far away is it? Is it as far as Oxford?
Laura You've seen maps.
Edmund No, I haven't.
Laura I have.
Emma See what I've done, Laura? See what I've saved fer your father? Your
two biggest mushrooms — 'cause of how he likes 'em so.

*Laura smiles. She and her mother embrace each other for a moment. There
is happy peace between them*

Edmund Mother. What's Oxford like?
Emma It's a girt big town where you can earn five and twenty shillings a
week and pay pretty near half in rent, so who'd want to go?
Edmund What do people do there?
Emma It's full of old buildings. It's where rich people's sons go to school,
when they've grown up.
Edmund What do they learn?
Emma Latin and Greek and suchlike, I suppose.
Edmund Do they all go there?
Emma No. Some go to Cambridge.
Edmund Which shall I go to, when I grow up?
Emma You'll have to go to work, my little man. Brains ain't no good to a
working chap. They make him discontented and saucy and lose him jobs.

*She takes her mats and rugs outside the cottage and beats them. Other
women are doing the same*

Morning, Mrs Blaby.

Mrs Blaby Morning, Mrs Timms.
Emma Morning, Mrs Peverill.
Mrs Peverill Morning.
Emma Think the weather's going to hold?
Mrs Blaby Until they get 'un all in?
Emma Ay.
Mrs Peverill Bound to, my husband says.
Edmund (*watching his mother hard at work*) Mother: why does God
sometimes send bad weather?
Emma Questions, Edmund, questions! You may not have school to go to but
I've still to beat and scrub, so go play while you can. Laura. Go play with
him.

Laura and Edmund wander past the hard-working women

Laura Oh, look! What's that plant called, Mrs Peverill?
Mrs Peverill 'Tis called "Mind Your Own Business" and I think I'd better
give a slip of it to your mother to put up for you!

Laura wheels her hoop away. Edmund follows

Ask me, I'd say children should be seen and not heard.
Mr Blaby Time she was earning her own living.
Mrs Peverill Come next harvest, she will be.
Mrs Blaby Not much to look at, is she: like a moll heron, all legs and wings.

SCENE 3

*Old Sally comes out of her cottage. She is a tall, broad old woman, 80 years
old, with dark curls and a white, fringed cap*

Sally Laura! Laura! Coom up here!
Laura It's Old Sally. Come on.

The children go up to Old Sally

Morning, Sally.
Sally Morning Laura.

*Old Sally's husband Dick is there, a dry, little withered old man with a smock
rolled up around his waist and trousers gartered with buckled straps. Sally
is by far the dominating partner but Dick is gleefully happy*

Laura Morning, Dick.
Dick Morning, Laura.
Laura Oh, Sally, what a good smell!
Sally I been brewin', haven't I?
Edmund Oh, Laura, look at those roses!
Dick York and Lancaster, they call 'em. Them's better 'n any o' yer oil paintings. Eh?
Sally Dick, show young Edmund here the grandfather clock.
Edmund Oh, please!
Dick Oh. Ay. Just as Sally says! Come on, only grandfather clock in the Rise.

Laura is not sure whether to follow Dick and Edmund or not. Sally motions her to stay

Sally Laura. You'm a good girl and I likes you. I know you'm good at readin' and writin', on account of how folks tries to pluck your feathers.
Laura But Dick can write, can't he?
Sally Oh, he could write ten words to us boys when they was in India, and I can make my name and that be all, so it's a bit okkard for business. (*Silence. She watches Laura*) Laura, ask me, I'd say you'm a girl might keep a secret.
Laura Oh, yes. Oh, yes, Sally.
Sally What do folks say 'bout me and Dick?

Laura hesitates

Go on! Don't flinch!
Laura They say they wish you'd tell them how 'tis done. How you live so comfortable when you're so old.
Sally (*laughing and clapping her hands*) Laura, when I were your age, all the land between here and the church were left by will to the poor o' the parish. All common land of turf and fuzz, 'twas then. But 'twere all stole away an' cut up into fields. Hundred Acre Field were common land. My grandfather owned this house and passed it on to my father. Us had a cow and pigs and a donkey cart and I drove the geese to the common. I know'd where the freshest grass growed, I can tell you. Us growed us own victuals and my mother made butter and at harvest time an' such like, my dad worked for wages. So us was happy. Not like country folks today, eh, raising great tribes o' children on ten shillin' a week wages? I didn't never hold wi' havin' a lot o' poor brats and nothin' to put in their bellies. Took us all us time to bring up us two and us had ... (*She checks. She has reached the main point of the conversation*) Us be swearin' you to secrecy, Laura.

Laura nods vigorously

Well. A-cause my father had a share o' common land he could make summat. And a-cause he made summat, he left summat. He left this house and seventy-five pound!

Laura gasps

Ay. An' me and Dick has saved every week for sixty year, even if it were no more nor a penny nor two pence. So that's how 'tis done.

Laura But why tell *me*, Sally?

Sally 'Cause we need letters write to seedsmen, an' postal orders fetched an' money added up. It be growed into more 'n poor old Dick's head can reckon. I watched him t'other night, poor old boy. It were like puttin' a poultice on a wooden leg. Will you help us?

Laura Yes. Can I? Oh, yes!

They embrace

Sally Dick. Dick. Here, Laura. Take your mother a bunch o' rosemary.

Dick and Edmund return

Edmund Oh, Laura, it's such a big clock, but the moon's broken.

Dick Ay, but we be abed early, so we don't miss him. Will 'er do it?

Sally Ay.

Dick I were a cat on hot bricks in there.

Sally (*giving Laura the rosemary*) Come tomorrow morning. Quick sharp.

Laura and Edmund go. Sally and Dick wave after them. Laura and Edmund wave and then walk on

Laura Edmund. Guess what!

Edmund What?

Laura When Sally was like me, she was a goose girl!

The band plays and sings Young Sally's song

Song

Band   Come softly, young Sally, and call the geese home
                 Call Lizzie, call Dripping, call Waddle-down-by
                 There's a great big black cloud full of snow in the sky
                 Come Sally, young Sally, and call the geese home.

Where's Sally, young Sally, who called the geese home
Where's Lizzie, where's Dripping, where's Waddle-down-
     by
Where are all the cold hailstones that fell from the sky
Where's Sally, young Sally, who drove the geese home.

Oh Sally, old Sally, who called the geese home
Where's Lizzie, where's Dripping who cackled all day
All gone like the fields that were stolen away
And Sally, young Sally, who drove the geese home.

All gone like the fields that were stolen away
And Sally, young Sally, who drove the geese home.

SCENE 4

*Emma has done her scrubbing and emptied the fireplace which she is now
cleaning, watched by Laura and Edmund*

Emma See this grate I'm cleaning? Looks done, doesn't it? But you watch.
(*She brushes vigorously*) There. That's the secret. Just that bit of extra
elbow grease after some folks would consider a thing done.
Laura Oh, Mother! Post, Mother! Here's Old Postie!

*Emma and other women come out of their houses. Old Postie is a gloomy,
grumpy man with flat feet. He has been forty years on this round and walks
with deliberate, rheumatic slowness*

Emma Look at him dawdle! You expecting something, Mrs Peverill?
Mrs Peverill No, I b'aint expecting nothing, but I be so yarning.
Old Postie (*stopping, looking through the letters and small parcels, to the
women outside the group of cottages*) No, I ain't got nothing for you, Mrs
Peverill. Your young Annie wrote to you only last week. She's got summat
else to do, besides sitting down on her arse in the servants' kitchen writin'
home all the time.
Mrs Peverill Now I call that real forrard language.
Old Postie Mrs Blaby. Parcel!
Emma Mrs Blaby!

Mrs Blaby comes out of her cottage

Mrs Blaby It's not summat for me, is it?

Old Postie 'Tis from your Aggie in London. Sent you her best dress, I'll be bound.

Mrs Blaby Well, better be out of the world than out of the fashion, b'aint that what they say?

Old Postie Oh, there is one for you, Mrs Peverill! And my! Ain't it a thin-roed 'un. Not much time to write to her mother these days. I took a good fat 'un from her to young Chad Gubbins.

Mrs Peverill Oh! — Don't he leave a sting behind him!

Old Postie waddles on. The women return to their homes. Emma takes her mats in with her

Edmund Mother, why are people in Lark Rise so poor?

Emma Poverty's no disgrace, Edmund, but 'tis a great inconvenience.

Laura sees something in the distance

Laura (*pointing*) What's that?

Emma Where?

Laura Coming from the turnpike.

Emma Oh yes. I see him. Driving too quick to be the fish cart.

Edmund It's the doctor's gig.

Emma So it is.

Laura Is anybody sick?

Emma If they were we'd have had the gossips round by this time in the morning — and Mrs Beamish hasn't come to her time yet.

Edmund He must be going to Fordlow.

Emma Ay. (*Her mind goes on to the next thing*) Now, Laura, you run round the Rise to poor Mr Sharman, there's a good girl, and ask him could he fancy a bit of cold bacon for his dinner.

Laura goes to the cottage of Sharman who is known as the Major because he served in the army. He is old and ill and has just dressed and with great difficulty dragged his chair to the fire

Laura Mr Sharman! Morning, Mr Sharman.

Sharman Uh? Oh. It's you, Laura.

Laura My mother says, could you fancy a bit of bacon for your dinner?

Sharman I'm cold.

Laura Sun's shining, Mr Sharman.

Sharman I'm cold.

The Doctor and the local Carrier have got out of the gig. They walk past the end house

Emma Morning, Doctor.
Doctor Morning, Mrs Timms.
Emma No trouble, I hope?
Doctor No, no. We've just come for Mr Sharman.
Emma Oh no! (*She knows exactly what they mean*)
Sharman Dunno where I'd be without your mum, Laura.
Laura Would you fancy some bacon?
Sharman I had bacon every day in the army.
Laura What shall I tell her, then?
Sharman I'm cold.
Laura It's coming up very hot, Mr Sharman.

The Doctor and the Carrier march in

Doctor Morning, Major. Come along, now.
Sharman Eh? What?
Doctor It's a nice morning. We've come to take you for a drive.
Sharman A drive? I've not driven nowhere since I left the hospital. Where
   to?
Doctor Oh, just a drive.
Sharman You'd not put me in the workhouse?
Doctor You'll feel better for the sunshine.
Sharman I won't go. I can look after myself.
Doctor No, you can't, and you've no family to do it for you.
Sharman I'm a soldier. I'll not die in no workhouse.
Doctor Come along, old chap.

*They lift Sharman up. He tries to resist but is too weak. They hustle his coat
round his shoulders*

Sharman Let me be.
Doctor That's the way. Put your shawl on.

*As the Doctor and Carrier walk Sharman slowly away the band sings "John
Barleycorn"*

Song

Band   There were three men come out of the West,
                    The victory to try,
                    And these three men they made a vow,
                    John Barleycorn should die.

They ploughed, they sowed, they harrowed him in,
Throwed clods all on his head,
And these three men rejoicing went,
John Barleycorn was dead.

They rode him round and round the field,
Till they came into a barn,
And there they made a solemn vow,
On little John Barleycorn.

They hired men with the crab tree sticks
To cut him skin from bone,
But the miller he served him worse than that,
For he ground him between two stones.

Doctor It's all for the best.

Everyone sings

All   All good gifts around us
Are sent from heaven above,
So thank the Lord, O thank the Lord,
For all His love.

SCENE 5

*Laura's Grandfather is a tall, old man with snow white hair and beard and
blue eyes. He wears an old-fashioned, close-fitting black overcoat and a
bowler hat. He moves slowly and painfully because rheumatism is gradually
seizing up his joints. He is carrying a gift of freshly cut flowers from his
garden*

*To reach the end house Grandfather must pass Queenie's cottage. Queenie
Macey is a little, wrinkled, yellow-faced old woman in a lilac sunbonnet. She
is dozing on a chair in the sun*

Grandfather Morning, Queenie, and how are you this — fast asleep, God
bless her.

*Queenie's husband Twister pops up from behind the hedge. He is a small,
thin-legged, jackdaw-eyed old fellow dressed in an old velveteen coat that
once belonged to a gamekeeper, a peacock's feather stuck in the band of his*

battered old bowler, and a red and yellow handkerchief knotted under one ear. He, too, has rheumatism and is slowly becoming the slack-witted person that he has often pretended to be. He has a big, open clasp-knife in one hand

Twister Why should God bless her? Why should he? I'll wake 'un up fer 'ee.
Grandfather No need for that, Twister, thank 'ee kindly.
Twister Her be my wife and un'll do what I says.
Grandfather What was you a-doing behind that hedge?
Twister Nothing. I caught a frog. Sun's shining, ain't it?
Grandfather You let that frog go, Twister, d'you hear?
Twister I did. I did let 'un go. But first I cut him front legs off. (*He thinks that this is both daring and funny*)
Grandfather Lord have mercy, Twister. Lord have mercy. (*He walks slowly on*)
Emma (*seeing him, going to meet him*) Why, Father: you've not walked round the Rise for a week or more.

Grandfather gives her the flowers

Oh, Dad. From your garden? Thank you. It just makes me think, if only I had thirty shillings a week regular I could keep everything so nice and tidy and keep *such* a table.

Grandfather sits painfully. Emma gets a flower jar

Grandfather Poor old Twister, eh? Poor Twister.
Emma There's some thinks he'd be better put away — but there he is, he still goes beating at shoots and he still earns a shilling or two opening farm gates for the brewery salesman's gig.
Grandfather I've known him forty year and he was allus the same. Whatever he dies on, he won't kill hisself with hard work (*He notices that something is wrong*) Emmie? Emmie, you b'aint crying, be you?
Emma Oh, Father! (*She weeps. Then she hears the children, and pulls herself together*)

Laura and Edmund come in

Laura Oh, Mother. Mother, they've taken Mr Sharman away.
Emma I know. I saw them.
Grandfather We all saw 'em — except your Granny. She wouldn't look.
Laura Why not? What was she doing?
Grandfather Reading.
Edmund What? What was she reading?

Emma Don't ask questions!
Grandfather Now, Emmie ... She were reading one of those what-d'you-call'ems, Edmund — novelettes. All about dukes and duchesses. When you say your prayers tonight, ask the Lord to help Mr Sharman.
Edmund D'you ever pray for your old fiddle?
Grandfather My old fiddle?
Edmund Didn't that get taken away?
Laura It had to be sold when Granny was ill.
Grandfather I got five pound for it.
Laura Did you miss it?
Grandfather I did, my maid, more than anything I've ever had to part with, and that's not a little, and I miss it still and always shall. But it went for a good cause and we can't have everything we want in this world. It wouldn't be good for us.
Laura Why not? I'd call it very good for you to have your old fiddle.
Emma Laura. Don't answer back.
Laura It's always money that causes people's troubles.
Emma Laura!
Grandfather If it *were* just money, Laura, life 'ud be simple.
Emma Now then, Laura, here's a penny. You go wait for Jerry Parish and you buy three oranges.

The children are delighted. They rush out

I'm sorry, Father. They've so many questions.
Grandfather They'll find the answers in the Bible and their own good time.
Emma How's your rheumatics?
Grandfather Bad.
Emma Is this walk too much for you?

Grandfather gestures. He does not want to admit it easily, but the walk is too far

I'll visit you. You save yourself for your garden.
Grandfather It's run wild since I can't stoop so much. (*Silence*) Your uncle's well. He sends you kind regards.
Emma He's a good man.
Grandfather To send me money? Ay. He is.
Emma But you'd send it to him if you'd prospered.
Grandfather (*watching her*) What about you, Emmie? Do you prosper?
Emma (*shaking her head*) Every year Albert says we'll give notice and move to Candleford. We'll go when we've killed the pig, he says. Then when we've killed the pig he'll say we'll go at Michaelmas. But we won't. . .

Grandfather Do you want to leave the Rise?
Emma I want him to be happy. I don't want him always coming home late
from public houses. (*She almost cries again*) You're good to me, Father.
You're so good.
Grandfather Well, you've always brought me your troubles, haven't you?

*Emma kneels in front of him: a little girl again. Grandfather smiles and, a bit
awkwardly because of his rheumatism, wipes her eyes*

Emma Oh, Father ...
Grandfather Sssh ...
Emma I'm sorry. I don't want to flinch. (*She blows her nose*)
Grandfather That's better. That's better. Now, you're going to be my own
brave little wench. And remember, my dear, there's one above who knows
what's best for us, even though we may not see it ourselves at the time.

Emma kisses him. There is great love between them

Now help me up.

Emma helps him up. It hurts. He smiles ruefully. He starts to go

Emma How long did you have that violin, Father?
Grandfather Oh — fifty-year. It's no use to me now. My fingers is too stiff
to play it. (*He seems to be going but turns again*) Of course, when I bought
it I was still a sinner. I hadn't seen Jesus, face to face. I were an eggler of
course but I didn't have the horse. I walked to buy eggs and carry 'em to
market. Oh, I strode out, Emmie. I was a brisk young sinner I can tell you
and I'd take my fiddle with me and play it at fairs. Folks 'ud dance and sing
all night and I'd laugh and play for 'em all night.

*He shakes his head and walks slowly away to the accompaniment of a lively
fiddle tune*

SCENE 6

*Jerry Parish arrives, ringing the bell of his fish cart, to be met by women of
the hamlet*

Jerry Come on now, Mrs Peverill. Bloaters, a penny each. Oranges, three
a penny.

Mrs Peverill I've threepence till my man gets his money.

Jerry Have a bloater.

Mrs Peverill But I've the children, Jerry. Mind you, I've some bread. Show me one wi' plenty of soft roe. I could spread it for them.

Mrs Beamish Morning, Jerry.

Jerry Morning, Mrs Beamish. Lor' blime me! Never knowed such a lot in my life for soft roes. Good job I ain't soft-roed or I should have got aten up myself afore now! (*He feels the bloater*) Oozin' — simply oozin' with goodness, I tell ye! But what's the good of one bloater among the lot of ye? Tell you what I'll do. I'll put you in these whoppers for twopence-halfpenny.

Mrs Peverill No.

Jerry Tell you what. Have three oranges. When you've eaten 'em, dry the peel on the hob, then the children chews on it or swaps it for conkers.

Mrs Peverill No, Jerry. If I've any money over I've got to put it to a new pair of boots for our George.

Jerry Lor' blime me, Mrs Peverill. I don't know why you come out here.

Mrs Peverill To have a look and a bit of a chat, Jerry. Why else?

Mrs Miller I'll have a bloater.

Jerry What's that, Mrs Miller?

Mrs Miller I've worked that hard this morning. I just fancy a bit o' summat.

Jerry This bloater's more'n a bit, Mrs Miller. It's three-haporth worth for a penny.

Laura (*it's not her turn*) Oh, look, Edmund! Mr Parish, what are those red and yellow things?

Jerry Love apples, my dear. Love apples they be, although some hignorant folks be a-calling them tommytoes. But you don't want any o' they— nasty sour things they be, as only gentry can eat.

Laura They look beautiful.

Jerry They'll only make 'ee sick. What's it to be? Three oranges?

Laura Please. Oh. What's that?

Jerry That fish? That's a John Dory, my dear. See them black marks? Looks like finger marks don't 'em? An' they do say that they be finger marks. He made 'em, that night, ye know, when they was fishin', ye know, and he took some and cooked 'em all ready for 'em an' ever since they say that ivery John Dory as comes out of the sea have got his finger marks on 'em.

Laura Do you mean the Sea of Galilee?

Jerry That's it, my dear. That's what they say; whether true or not, of course, I *don't* know, but there be the finger marks right enough, and that's what they say in our trade.

Song

Jerry   I've red tommytoes for the gentry
                 I've bloaters for the likes of you
                 I've pears and I've peaches a-plenty
                 And an orange for the likes of you

                 I've a bunch of grapes for the gentry
                 And bloaters for the likes of you
                 I can tip my hat most politely
                 And be patient with the likes of you

                 There's one kind of fish that is saintly
                 And he's taught me a thing or two
                 It's red tommytoes for the gentry
                 And patience for the likes of you

All   Yes it's red tommytoes for the gentry
                 And it's patience for the likes of us!

Song

Band   Are you there John Dory
                 Are you there
                 In Cottesloe Pond?
                 Are you there John Dory
                 Are you there
                 In Cottesloe Pond?

                 Are you there John Dory
                 Are you there
                 In Cottesloe Pond?
                 Are you there in glory
                 Are you there
                 In Cottesloe Pond?
                 Are you there John Dory
                 Are you there?

Jerry passes on to his next place of call

ACT II
Scene 1

It is midday. Old Twister, realizing that Queenie is still asleep and that Emma is alone again, sidles up to the end house and calls her

Twister Hey, missus. Missis Timms.

Emma jumps

Did you know that twenty year ago, I used to sell nuts on market days?
Emma Yes. Queenie told me.
Twister Bassalonie nuts. Do you want to see 'em?
Emma How can I see them, Twister, if it was twenty years ago?
Twister Oh you can see 'em, missus. Here they be! (*He lets his trousers fall and exposes himself*) Bassalonies big as ponies!
Emma Twister, you ought to be ashamed of yourself doing that again.
Twister Bassalonies big as ponies!
Queenie (*waking up*) Twister! You disgusting old fool, you!

Twister is dismayed. He clutches at his trousers and runs away

Look at him. Slack-twisted old fool. Run away at the sight of me. As well 'a might. Still remembers the pie, don't he? Did I tell 'ee about the pie?
Emma You did, Queenie. But it can bear telling again.
Queenie Well. 'Twere forty-five year ago. He came home drunk and took the strap off his trousers and he beat me. I went to bed sobbin', I did. Next morning he gets up, but no strap. Nor nowhere to be found. So he holds his trousers up wi' string and goes to work. Well — when he come home for tea, I baked a pie. I'd done a tulip on top and it were baked just beautiful. "You cut it," I says, "I made it a-purpose for you. Come, don't 'ee be afraid on it. 'Tis all for you." Then I turns my back on him and looks in the cupboard and he cuts the pie and there inside on it is the strap, all curled up. Twister went white as a ghost an' got up an' went out. But it cured 'em for's not so much as laid a finger on me from that day to this! And I hope a-Saturday he comes home wi' a shillin' or two, for if he don't there be no tea for him and no snuff for me neither. (*She takes out her snuffbox*) Look at 'un. Clean empty and I can't do wi'out my pinch o'snuff. 'Tis meat an' drink to me. (*She sniffs deeply at the empty box*) Ah! That's better. The

ghost o' good snuff's better nor nothing. Mrs Timms, my dear, if I had a pound a week coming in, I 'udn't care if it rained hatchets and hammers!

Queenie and Emma laugh

Emma How are the bees, Queenie?
Queenie Poor little craturs.
Emma You ain't still waiting for the last swarm?
Queenie I am. They was almost frozed in winter. I wanted to gather them up, take them indoors, and set them in rows in front of a good fire, and then there were all that rain and as you know, Mrs Timms, a swarm in July ain't worth a fly so I'll not have too much for the honey-man. That's why I need Twister, for all his disgustin' carryin'-ons. Come winter I'll need every shillin' he can earn.

They both start at the noise they hear

That's it. That's the little craturs swarming.
Emma There they go. Down your sweet-pea alley.

Queenie rushes home and picks up her pitchfork and an iron spoon

Emma Queenie. Hurry, Queenie. They're buzzing over into Master Tuffrey's.
Queenie (*rushing after the bees, banging the spoon on the back of the pitchfork*) I'm after 'em, Mrs Timms. I'm after 'em!

SCENE 2

Martha's mother Mrs Beamish is heavily pregnant. During the following scene Mrs Beamish plaits Martha's long hair into an inverted saucer at the back of her head. Laura watches and Edmund stands where he can follow what is happening but not be part of it

Mrs Beamish Martha, will you please keep still! Now you know where this big house is, don't you Martha?
Martha I can ask on the way.
Mrs Beamish It's four miles walking. And when you get there you speak proper and you answer "Yes, mum", all polite like.
Martha Yes, mum.
Mrs Beamish Keep still!
Martha How will it look?

Mrs Beamish Like a scarecrow if you don't keep still.
Laura Have you had it plaited up before, Martha?

Martha shakes her head excitedly

Mrs Beamish Keep still, Martha! And don't go undoing it on the way nor nothing like that. You say you're Martha Beamish and you're twelve years old, and you've just left school and you're looking for your pretty place to learn service in. It's a big house. It's not a farmhouse. Once a farmhouse servant allus a farmhouse servant but this is a big house and you'll be growing strong enough for proper gentlemen's service. Understand?
Martha Yes, Ma. How do it look?
Mrs Beamish You'll see soon enough. If I hadn't felt sick as a dog this morning, I would have come with you even if my time is near.
Martha I know you would, Ma.
Mrs Beamish How about asking Laura if she'll go with you? Keep still. It's company, isn't it?
Martha Oh, can I, Ma? Would you like that, Laura?
Laura Yes.
Mrs Beamish Will it suit your mother?
Laura Yes.
Mrs Beamish What you *must* do, Martha, and you must see as she does, Laura, is when the lady asks you, say I've not a penny to spend on your outfit.
Martha Not a penny.
Mrs Beamish So will her send me your first month's wages in a-hadvance to buy necessities. Understand?
Martha Yes.
Mrs Beamish Laura?
Laura Yes. I'd best go for my dinner now.
Mrs Beamish Ay. You had.
Martha Oh, how do it look, Ma?
Mrs Beamish Come in and I'll show 'ee.

Edmund is waiting for Laura. They walk along in silence and then he speaks

Edmund Mother won't let you walk four miles.
Laura I shan't tell her.
Edmund She'll find out.
Laura Oh, be quiet, Edmund.
Edmund You can't walk that far.
Laura Yes I can. I want to see a big house.

Laura is about to admonish him when they see Queenie pass by in the distance still tanging her bees

Queenie I'm still after the little craturs. I'm still after them. (*She disappears*)
Laura (*turning back to Edmund*) You can't walk that far.
Edmund Shall I ask Mother if I can?
Laura (*impasse, having to give way*) Just you keep up with us, that's all.
Edmund Course I will. There's the squire.
Laura Where?
Edmund There. Going home from his shooting.

SCENE 3

Squire Bracewell has a gun and haversack and a brace of dead rabbits. He is a jovial, red-faced, middle-aged bachelor and lives at the hall with his widowed mother. They are not so well off as they once were. Bracewell is a simple sincere person who is on the whole well liked in the village and hamlet. On his way, he meets John Price, the son of Old Price. He has just finished his five years' army service and is dressed in a red infantry jacket

Squire I say. John Price. It is John Price, isn't it?
Price Yes, sir. John Price, sir.
Squire Just got your discharge?
Price Yes, sir.
Squire How many years was it?
Price Five.
Squire Good Lord. I remember you at the schoolroom concert. Five years.
  Good Lord. You were in the Sudan, weren't you?
Price Yes, sir.
Squire Good Lord.

There is a little awkward silence

Price I see you're still out with your gun, sir.
Squire Oh yes. I never miss a day.
Price I hopes your mother be keeping well, sir.
Squire Thank you, Price. Thank you. She is. She's looking older of course,
  but ...

There is another awkward silence

  Speaking of the annual schoolroom concert, you were one of my stalwarts,
  you know.

Price I did my bit, sir.
Squire You were jolly good. I still run the Black Minstrel Troupe.
Price I always enjoyed putting black on my face, sir.
Squire For the last couple of years, we've got up red and blue uniforms —
and we've got a new song.
Price Oh, ay?
Squire Would you like to hear it?
Price Yes please, sir!

Squire Bracewell sings the "Black Minstrel Song"

Song

Squire   A friend of Darwin's came to me
                    "A million years ago" said he
                    "You had a tail and no great toe"
                    I answered him "That may be so
                    But I've one now I'll have you know
                    G-r-r-r-r-r-out!"

(Making a kicking motion) And then I plant a great kick on Tom Binns's
backside.
Price Tom Binns?
Squire Yes. People seem to laugh more at him than at the others. We rehearse
once a week in the schoolroom. Are you going to volunteer again?
Price I'd be happy to, sir.
Squire Splendid. Thank you, Price. Thank you kindly. Blackie! Dot! Where
are those confounded dogs?
Price Er — a friend of *whose*, sir?
Squire What? Oh. Darwin's. "A friend of Darwin's came to me". Good-day.
Price Good-day to you, Mr Bracewell, sir.

"The Soldier's Song", sung by the men as they cross the field

Song

Men   Poor old soldier,
                    Poor old soldier,
                    If ever I 'list for a soldier again,
                    The devil shall be me Sergeant.

                    Poor old soldier,
                    Poor old soldier,

If ever I 'list for a soldier again,
The devil shall be me Sergeant.

Twopence I got for selling my cloak,
And twopence for selling my blanket,
If ever I 'list for a soldier again,
The devil shall be my Sergeant.

Poor old soldier,
Poor old soldier,
If ever I 'list for a soldier again,
The devil shall be me Sergeant.

SCENE 4

The line of mowers moves on across the field. Then when Boamer raises his hand both the line and the song stop

Boamer Master Price, what time be it by your old turnip watch?
Old Price Ten minutes after, Boamer.
Boamer I thought it must. Knock off for dinner hour, lads. Sit down and rest your backsides. But it won't be no hour. Half-hour exact and then back to it. Now where's Pumpkin with that yellow-stone jar? Pumpkin!

Answering shout

You bringing up the jar?

Another shout

Well, hurry up. And when you do, give the oldest first drink of ale.

The men throw themselves down on the ground and open their lunches. The food is wrapped in handkerchiefs. Some have bread and cold bacon, which they cut very neatly with clasp-knives. Some have bread and a bit of cheese. It is eagerly awaited relaxation. The men are hungry. Their conversation is punctuated by silences of rest and eating. Boamer sets up his hat with a stick and a long piece of string, as a bird trap

Old Price Well — us've made a good start, Boamer lad.
Bishie Ay. Us have. Good old Boamer.
Old Price Best start I've seen for twenty year.

Boamer We must keep at it and hope that the weather holds.
Pumpkin (*arriving from wheat field*) What you got there, Bishie lad?

Bishie holds up a piece of cheese and then pops it into his mouth, Pumpkin smiles

You've seen some hard days' work in these fields, Master Tuffrey.
Old David Ay.
Pumpkin What was the hardest?
Old David The hardest?
Old Price Ay. What *were* the hardest?
Old David Oh, the hardest were in Duffus Piece when farmer was a young man and he says, says he, "That field o' oats got to come in afore night, for there's a rain a-coming!" But we didn't flinch, not we! Got the last load under cover by midnight. A'most too fagged-out to walk home. But we didn't flinch. We done it!
Pumpkin I'll wager you done it, Master Tuffrey.
Old David Oh, we done it, Pumpkin! We done it!

Appreciative smiles and chuckles. They eat and pass the ale

Bishie Weren't it Duffus Piece where you a-faced up to the old bull, Master Price?
Old Price No, that were Fishponds.
Bishie O' course it were, Fishponds.

Old Price rests and reflects. They wait for him to tell the story

Old Price Old bull—he comes for me wi' his head down. But I didn't flinch. I ripped off a bit o' loose rail and went for he. 'Twas him as did the flinchin'!

Warm laughter and then silence

Bishie Now you lads with them cold pudding ends. Don't be gettin' that 'ere treacle in your ears.

The men are suitably amused

Old David Pass the jug, Pumpkin, thank'ee kindly.
Bishie Where's Old Monday Morning with that barrel?
Boamer Oh, he be riding round after dinner or I'll have strong words to say to him.
Old Price That you will, Boamer.

Laughter

You must be proud of him, David. Regular proud o' a son like him.
Old David Oh, ay.
Bishie Not fagged out, are you, Master Tuffrey?
Old David Half-fagged, Bishie. Half-fagged.
Pumpkin That's a good 'un. Half-fagged!

By now the men are finishing their food. They shake out the crumbs from their red handkerchiefs, and light their clay pipes with thick shag tobacco. Boamer shakes his crumbs under the hat

Boamer Now, you young boychaps — if you want to walk off and shoot your catapults 'tis the time to do it. But don't be making no nuisance for Mrs Spicer's gang and when you hear me a-shouting, come back here.
Pumpkin If you ask me, we'd a-get this corn in faster without them boys.
Old Price Ay. When it comes to work one boy's a boy, two boys be half a boy, and three boys be no boy at all.

Quiet laughter. They are enjoying the rest and their pipes

Pumpkin Look at that.
Old David Uh?
Pumpkin Yellowhammer — after them crumbs.

Concentrated silence as Boamer approaches the end of the string and pulls it to bring down the hat brim and trap the bird. He pulls it — but the bird has flown

Old Price Oh, never!
Boamer (*winding his string around the stick — for the next time*) It's a good cage bird, is a yellowhammer.
Old David Ay. If you catch him.

Silence. Then Old David gets up

Well — I be going up the hedge to relieve myself.
Bishie You know what they say, Master Tuffrey — eat well, work well, sleep well and shit well, once a day.

Appreciative laughter. Old David ambles away. There is a ruminative silence

Bishie (*singing*) "Adam catched Eve by the fur below. And that's the oldest catch we know".

Pumpkin That it be, Bishie.

Bishie I wonder why it don't say drink well once a day. Or come to that, you-know-what well once a day, eh, Pumpkin?

Pumpkin That's 'cause not even a well known old ram, like Mr Price here, could do that, not 'im, not with them bellies swelled out here with children.

Bishie Ay. 'Tis more like rolling off than rolling on, ain't it?

Boamer Look you out, Bishie, or some of them boys'll hear you.

Smothered laughter. Silence

Bishie Hear what 'tis said the rector asked Mrs Spicer?

Old Stut Sh-sh-shame on you, B-Bishie.

Pumpkin Oh, shut you up, Old Stut.

Bishie Rector says, "Morning there, Mrs Spicer, my good woma. Why be you wearing them trousers to go to your work afield? I thought you didn't have no unmentionables."

First laughter

Mrs Spicer says, "I don't know what you'm a-talking about, I'm sure. I thought the only unmentionable in your ears was Mr Gladstone."

Laughter

Pumpkin How many unmentionables have you got, Master Price?

Old Price I've enough for one lifetime, I can tell 'ee!

Bishie Well said, Master Price.

Old Price The brimstone's fair coming out of your young mouths this mornin'.

Boamer Ay. If you're not careful there'll be some wooman comin' along the road.

Pumpkin Ay. Oh, ay. 'Tis field talk when all's said and done.

Bishie does not really agree but he shuts up. A thoughtful silence. Sam Pridham sings "Sam's Song"

Song

Sam   As I was going to the fair of Athy
                I spied a girl's petticoat hung out to dry,

I took off my trousers,
And I hung them close by,
To keep that girl's petticoat warm.

The petticoat flapped
And it made a loud noise,
It flounced and it fluttered,
Lost feminine poise,
And it wound round the legs of my old corduroys.
Oh trousers, I hope you're on form!

Silence, each in his own thoughts

Old Price Ay. It were thirty year ago, when I faced that old bull at Fishponds.
(*Short silence*) It were the year my brother James married that Candleford
woman. By hem, but she were near! She were that near she 'udn't give
away enough to make a pair of legging for a skylark.

Quiet laughter

Pumpkin What became of her, Master Price?
Old Price Dead, Pumpkin, lad. Stone dead.

Silence

Boamer What does your old watch say now, Master Price?
Old Price (*getting his watch out*) Half an hour on, Boamer.
Boamer (*standing to call his men back to work*) All my gang back here!
Follow your King of the Mowers!

*The gang re-forms to the "Harvest Work Song", mows a swath and passes
on*

Song

Men   When harvest comes on and the reaping begins,
The farmer the fruit of the earth gathers in.
In mirth let us talk till the season be gone,
And at night give a holler till it's all of a row, till it's all of
a row,
And at night give a holler till it's all of a row.

Then early next morning our hooks we do grind,
And away to the cornfields to reap and to bind.
Our foreman looks back and he leaves well behind,
And he gives a loud holler, bring it all well behind, bring it
    all well behind,
And he gives a loud holler, bring it all well behind.

O then says the foreman, behind and before,
We will have a fresh whet and half a pint more.
So me jolly boys to the end we will go,
To the end we will go till it's all of a row, till it's all of a row,
To the end we will go till it's all of a row.

When night it comes on to the farm we will steer,
To partake a good supper and to drink a strong beer.
In wishing the farmer such blessings in his life,
And in drinking a health unto him and his wife, unto him
    and his wife,
And in drinking a health unto him and his wife.

Our wheat is all in, oats, barley are bound,
Here's success to the farmer who ploughs through the
    ground,
As for this wheat stubble into turnips we'll sow,
And so we'll continue till it's all of a row, till it's all of a row,
And so we'll continue till it's all of a row.

ACT III
SCENE 1

The women and children have also had their meagre dinners. Now the women sit outdoors with their babies or their sewing or a novelette

Emma and Mrs Peverill sit quietly and happily in the sun. Laura and Edmund come up to their mother and kiss her

Emma Where are you off to?
Laura Walking with Martha Beamish. Up to the turnpike.
Emma And Edmund?
Edmund Yes, Mother.
Emma Mind you're back before the cooking smoke goes up.
Laura Yes, Mother.

Laura and Edmund go. Mrs Peverill, who has been awaiting the right moment to start a conversation calls across to Emma

Mrs Peverill 'Tis a good read I have 'ere, Mrs Timms. 'Tis one o' them where the lady loves a gamekeeper. But if you ask me him's a duke in disguise.

Emma smiles and nods. She too likes a good story but she does not wish to talk about this one

Lord save us!
Emma What from?
Mrs Peverill Mrs Andrews coming round for a gossip.

Mrs Andrews has no children still at home, which is why she has the time and the loneliness to be a gossip

Mrs Andrews Afternoon, Mrs Peverill. Afternoon, Mrs Timms.
Emma Afternoon, Mrs Andrews. Won't you sit down?
Mrs Andrews No. Oh, no, thank 'ee. I mustn't stop a minute.
Mrs Peverill Think weather's a-goin' to hold?
Mrs Andrews It's not weather as worries me so much as Mrs Beamish.
Emma Mrs Beamish?

Mrs Andrews But a day or two off her time and not a stitch put into a rag yet.

Emma Oh, Mrs Andrews, I'm sure she's plenty left over from her last baby.

Mrs Andrews I been a-watching her clothes-line. Not a new bit o'sewing come out there.

Mrs Peverill Well there's always the rector's daughter and the clothes box.

Mrs Andrews Oh, ay: and a slut's work is never done. And as for that young Jim Shaw — well, you knows what I've allus said about *him*.

Silence. Mrs Andrews waits for a response. Emma won't give one and this inhibits Mrs Peverill. Mrs Andews has to continue

I seen a well-dressed man knockin' at their door to tell poor Mrs Shaw that young Jim's in trouble over money. I knows it for a fac'.

Silence

Emma Are you sure you won't sit down, Mrs Andrews?

Mrs Andews I mustn't stop a minute, Mrs Timms. Why here's Mistress Macey, poor old soul! They all be saying dreadful things about her Twister.

Silence

Have you seen that Polly Arless home on her holiday from service? And that Mary Mullins? If you ask me they looks in the family way, both on 'em!

Mrs Peverill I'm sure they b'ain't, Mrs Andrews.

Mrs Andrews I've sized 'em up, Mrs Peverill. And I'll tell 'ee another thing — and this I do know for a fac': young Teddy the Prince of Wales has given one of his fancy woomen a necklace with pearls, the size o' pigeons' eggs and the poor old Queen, God bless her, with her crown on 'er head and tears a-runnin' down her cheeks had to go down on her bended knees and a-beg him to turn the whole lot of saucy hussies out o' Windsor Castle.

Mrs Peverill Ooh! I call that shameful. And did him?

Mrs Andews Did him what?

Mrs Peverill Did him turn 'em out?

Mrs Andrews He refused. I know it for a fac'. I mustn't stop a minute longer. I only came out to borrow a spoonful o' tea from Mrs Ashley.

Mrs Andrews goes on her way round the Rise

Mrs Peverill Never sits down, do she?

Emma Mrs Andrews? No. Standing gossips always stay longest.

Mrs Peverill It's with her children havin' grown up. The wooman's got no
one to talk to. Still, I think she makes a bit of a change even when I do see
lies coming out of her mouth like steam.

Emma smiles. Silence

Emma How's your lace coming, Mrs Peverill?
Mrs Peverill Not like the old days, Mrs Timms. I only does it now to keep
my hand in. They've killed 'um with they Nottingham machines. Them
wer' the days — when I wer' a girl like your Laura, and we took a year's
work to Banbury Fair. Them wer' the days, Mrs Timms. Money to spend!
I bought calico and linsey-wolsey and that chocolate print I still got a piece
of on my old quilt, and pipes and packets o' shag for the men, and rag dolls
and ginger-bread and snuff and tripe.
Emma Tripe?
Mrs Peverill Tripe. Only time in the year we had it. I'd heat 'un up wi' an
onion an' a nice bit o' thickenin'. Then us had the elderberry wine, Mrs
Timms. Them wer' the days!

Silence. Emma works at her sewing

My wine were very good this year. I done a good lot o' coltsfoot and the
parsnip were real strong. My man likes that.

They sit quietly. Then Mrs Blaby comes out of her cottage

Afternoon, Mrs Blaby.
Mrs Blaby Mrs Peverill.
Emma Afternoon.
Mrs Blaby Afternoon, Mrs Timms. Well, I must say I feels all the better for
that. I locked my door and I washed up as far as possible and down as far
as possible.
Mrs Peverill What about possible itself?
Mrs Blaby I heard that, Mrs Peverill, and I'd call it men's talk.

*Mrs Peverill and Mrs Blaby laugh. Then they look at Emma, who has not
laughed, but who feels that she must nevertheless respond to them. They all
hear the sound of the skylark*

Emma I love this time of day.
Mrs Peverill Ay. It's a wooman's one bit o' rest.

Silence

Mrs Blaby Remember when my Aggie was home on her holidays last year and the dress on her were sky blue, wi' very wide sleeves?

Mrs Peverill That were the best dress come to the Rise last year.

Mrs Blaby She sent it in her parcel.

Mrs Peverill She never.

Mrs Blaby She did. I'll have to let 'un out o' course. But it be real dressy. I do love anything a bit dressy.

Mrs Peverill I'd call that summat to save for high days and holidays and bonfire night.

Mrs Blaby She sent a hat an' all.

Mrs Peverill Never.

Mrs Blaby Very wide brim it has.

Mrs Peverill That's the fashion, ain't it? I'd not be seen goin' to the privy in one of them chimney pot hats!

They all smile. Silence

Emma How old's your Aggie now, Mrs Blaby?

Mrs Blaby Sixteen. But I told her — I allus tells my gals — that if they goes gettin' themselves into trouble they'll have to go to the workhouse, for I won't have 'em at home.

Mrs Peverill So I tells mine. I think it's why I've had no trouble with 'em.

Silence

Mrs Blaby That Emily's baby, though. Ain't she a beauty?

Mrs Peverill They allus do say that that sort of child *is* the finest.

Mrs Blaby What I say is the wife ought to have the first child and the husband the second. Then there wouldn't ever be no more.

Silence

Mrs Peverill My, your complexion do look fine, Mrs Timms.

Emma I wash my face in rainwater.

Mrs Blaby That's it then.

Silence

Mrs Peverill How about a cup o' tay?

Mrs Blaby Ay.

Mrs Peverill Cup o' tay, Mrs Timms?

Emma No, thank you, I think I'll just go inside for a bit of a lie down.

She goes inside

Mrs Blaby She's a bit la-di-da, that Mrs Timms.
Mrs Peverill Well, she's in with all them young married ones.
Mrs Blaby She's expecting again, ain't she?
Mrs Peverill Ay.
Mrs Blaby Not that she falls out with nobody.
Mrs Peverill Can't afford to, can us, in a place as small as this 'un?
Mrs Blaby Come on. I'll ask Mrs Miller to have that cup o' tay with us.

SCENE 2

Laura, Edmund, Martha and the Lady Band Singer now come on singing and playing "The Old Woman from Cumberland"

Song

Chorus	Here comes an old woman from Cumberland
	With all her children in her hand
	And please do you want a servant today?
Edmund	What can they do? What can they do?
Chorus	This can brew and this can bake
	This can make a wedding cake
	This can wear a gay gold ring
	This can sit in the barn and sing
	This can go to bed with a king
	And this one can do everything.
Edmund	Oh I will have that one
	Yes I will have that one

Edmund selects someone and they have a tug-of-war

Chorus	Goodbye, Mother, Goodbye.

One side wins. They then play the game two more times, first with additional members of the company, and, for the final time, with members of the audience as well. Then there is a crashing electric chord from the band

Edmund We can't go down here.
Laura This is the way.
Edmund We can't go.
Martha Why can't we?
Edmund 'Cause that's the witch elder.
Laura What?

Edmund There. By the brook.

They look

Laura So 'tis. 'Tis the witch elder.
Martha We can walk past it.
Laura Are you sure?
Martha Course I am. 'Tis only if the tree's cut that it bleeds human blood.
Laura Do you believe that?
Martha No. I don't believe in the beast's pond, neither.
Laura I've seen it.
Martha My father says there's no such pond.
Edmund Oh, yes, there is.
Martha There isn't.
Laura There is. But Queenie says that no-one living's seen the monster.
Edmund But people did see.
Laura Course they did.
Edmund It's as big as a bullock but slimy, like a newt.
Martha I don't believe none of it.
Edmund If you don't believe, Martha, you cut the elder tree.
Martha I — I ain't got no knife, have I? So I can't cut it, can I?
Edmund I'll find a stone.

The band plays and sings "Witch Elder"

Song

Band   Get up get up my father cried
                  For the witch is in my bed
                  She's in my bed and in my head
                  And in the candle flame

The music continues

Martha How could she be in a tree?
Laura Because she was an old woman who lived in the Rise. Men and boys
    chased her with pitch-forks until she reached the brook. Well, witches can't
    cross running water so she turned herself into this elder tree. Next morning
    there was the old woman fetching water from the well and here was this tree
    that hadn't been there before standing by the brook.
Edmund (*he has found a sharp stone*) Here's one. You could cut with this
    one.

The band sings

> Don't cut the tree my father cried
> For the witch is in the leaves
> She's in the leaves and in the sheaves
> And in the cloudless sky ...

The music stops abruptly. Martha must decide what to do

Martha What if the tree really bleeds? What if the witch comes out and runs after us?

Another crashing chord. The children run round the space. Then they are confronted by Garibaldi Jacket. She lives in a large manor house and is young and slight with a dead white face, arched brows and hair brushed straight back from her forehead. She wears a scarlet Garibaldi jacket and a black shirt

Martha Please, mum — do you want a maid?
Garibaldi Yes. Do you want a place?
Martha Yes, mum.
Garibaldi What's your name?
Martha Martha Beamish, mum.
Garibaldi How old are you?
Martha Twelve.
Garibaldi What can you do?

Martha is not sure. She looks at Laura. Laura is not sure, either

Can you do what you're told?
Martha Yes, mum.
Garibaldi Well that sounds right. This isn't a hard place because although there are sixteen rooms only three or four of them are in use. Can you get up at six without being called?
Martha Yes, mum.
Garibaldi There's the kitchen range to light and the flues to be swept once a week, the dining-room to be swept and dusted and the fire lit before breakfast. I'm down myself in time to prepare breakfast. No cooking's required, beyond preparing vegetables.
Martha Yes, mum.
Garibaldi After breakfast you'll help me with the beds and turning out the rooms and paring the potatoes and so on; and after dinner there's plenty to do — washing-up, cleaning knives and boots and polishing silver.
Martha Yes, mum.
Garibaldi There'll be more jobs in the evening of course but at nine o'clock you'll be free to go to bed — after placing hot water in my bedroom.

Martha Yes, mum.

Garibaldi Then, as wages, I can offer you two pounds ten a year. It is not a great wage but you are very small and you'll have an easy place and a comfortable home. You won't feel lonely, will you?

Martha No, mum.

Garibaldi Tell your mother I shall expect her to fit you out well. You will want caps and aprons. I like my maids to look neat. And tell her to let you bring plenty of changes, for we only wash once in six weeks. I have a woman to do it all up.

Laura looks at Martha because she remembers what Mrs Beamish said. But Martha is bewildered

Martha Yes, mum.

Garibaldi Well, I shall expect you next Monday, then.

Martha Yes, mum.

Garibaldi Good. Now. Are you all hungry?

Martha Yes, mum.

Edmund Oh, yes, mum.

Garibaldi Then let's see what there is in the pantry.

ACT IV
SCENE 1

It is evening

The Cheapjack arrives at Lark Rise with his cart of crockery and tinware and a rigged-up back-cloth painted with icebergs and penguins and polar bears. He lights a naptha flare and clashes his basins together like bells. People gather round him

Cheapjack Come buy! Come buy! Look at these bargains! Twenty-one pieces of a tea service and not a flaw in any one of them! The Queen has its fellow in Buckingham Palace!

Mrs Peverill Mrs Timms! Mrs Timms! 'Tis a cheapjack!

Cheapjack Look at this! Look! Twenty-one pieces! And look at this! Just listen to the music of this chamber pot! (*He rings the pot with his knuckles*) Sweet music in the night! Sweet music!

Mrs Miller Oh what forrard jokes!

Cheapjack You don't like jokes, missis? You don't like humorosity? I'll give you a song.

He sings and the band plays the "Cheapjack Song"

Song

> There was a man in his garden walked
> And cut his throat with a lump of chalk
> His wife, she knew not what she did
> She strangled herself with the saucepan lid.

Chorus

> In and out the windows
> In and out the windows
> In and out the windows
> Until the break of day

Cheapjack

> There was a man and a fine young fellow
> Who poisoned himself with an umbrella
> Even Joey in his cot
> Shot himself dead with a chamber pot

Chorus   In and out the windows
                   In and out the windows
                   In and out the windows
                   Until the break of day

Cheapjack   When you hear this horrible tale
                   It makes your faces all turn pale
                   Your eyes go green, you're overcome
                   So tweedle tweedle tweedle tum.

The song is well liked. It launches the Cheapjack into his patter

(*Speaking*) Two bob! Only two bob for this handsome set of jugs! Here's one for your beer and one for your milk and another in case you break one of the other two. Nobody's willing to speculate?

The men return from work in the fields, singing

Song

Men   Our oats they're hoed
                   And our barley's reaped
                   Our hay it is mowed
                   And our hovels heaped.

                   Come boys come, come boys come,
                   We'll merrily roar out harvest home.
                   Harvest home, harvest home.
                   We'll merrily roar out harvest home.

                   We've cheated the parson
                   We'll cheat him again,
                   Why should the old bugger
                   Have one in ten?

                   One in ten, one in ten,
                   Why should the old bugger have one in ten?
                   Harvest home, harvest home,
                   We'll merrily roar out harvest home.

Cheapjack   Then what about this 'ere set of trays straight from Japan and the peonics hand-painted? Or this lot of basins, exact replicas of the one the Princess of Wales supped her gruel from when Prince George was born. Why, damme, they cost me more'n two bob!

By now the men have arrived and stand wearily round the cart

I could get twice the two bob I'm asking here in Banbury tomorrow. But I'll give 'em to you — for at two bob you can't call it selling — because I like your faces and my load's so heavy the horse refused to pull it. Alarming bargains! Tremendous sacrifices! Come buy! Come buy! Three-pence for a large pudding basin! A dozen tumblers and a ball of string! Sixpence for a tin saucepan! Wooden spoons! A penny nutmeg grater! Come buy! Come buy! Never let it be said that this place — what's it called?

Laura Lark Rise.

Cheapjack Lark Rise. Never let it be said that Lark Rise is the poverty-strickenest place on God's earth! Here! Good dinner-plates for you! Every one a left-over from a first-class service. Buy one of these and you'll have the satisfaction of knowing that you're eating off the same ware as lords and dukes! Only three halfpence each! Who'll buy? Who'll buy?

One or two women buy

That's better! That's more like old England! Now look at these, you men home from work. Look at this tea service. You just look at the light through it. (*He hands out pieces of crockery*) And you, madam. And you, sir. Ain't it lovely china, thin as an eggshell, practically transparent and with every one of them roses handpainted with a brush. You can't let a set like that go out of the place now can you? I can see all your mouths a-watering. All run home and bring out them stockings from under your mattresses and the first one to get back shall have it for twelve bob!

Silence. Nobody moves

Pumpkin Twelve bob? By hem! We ain't got twelve pence.

There is slightly ashamed laughter from the crowd

Mrs Peverill I don't like it. It ain't good to look poor as well as bein' poor.

Cheapjack Oh, come on then. It *is* poverty-stricken. Hand them pieces back. I won't shame you.

People hand the pieces back. At the same time they do feel ashamed. Then John Price, the returned soldier, speaks up

Price How much did you say, mister? Twelve bob? I'll give you ten.

Pumpkin Wert up, John, lad! No flinchin'!

Price I'll give you ten bob.
Cheapjack Can't be done, matey. Cost me more nor that. (*He looks at John
   Price's girl Polly*) For her bottom drawer, is it?
Price Ay.
Cheapjack Then I tell you what I will do. You give me eleven and six and
   I'll throw in this handsome silver-gilt vase for your mantelpiece.
Price Done.

*Music again. Applause. The hamlet's good name is saved. People help John
Price to carry off his tea service*

SCENE 2

At the end house Emma gives the children their tea

Emma You deserve a darn good bommicking, that's what you deserve.
Laura No, we don't.
Emma Yes, you do. You told me you were going up the turnpike, but you
   went with Martha to see about her petty place, didn't you?
Laura Yes.
Emma Yes, well Mrs Beamish couldn't go but you did and that was very
   thoughtful, but telling me a lie was sinful. You can lock up from a thief but
   you can't from a liar. Well, what have you got to say for yourself?
Edmund It was a waste of time.
Emma What?
Edmund Martha forget to ask for her wages in advance so her mother won't
   let her go. And anyway, they say it's a haunted house.
Emma Edmund, if you aren't a better boy, old Oliver Cromwell will have
   you.

Edmund does not seem very hungry

Edmund. Eat up.

No response

Edmund.
Edmund Please, Mother, I'm not very hungry.
Emma You walked far enough.
Edmund The lady at the big house gave us roast beef.
Emma Did she now?
Edmund I had four helpings.

Emma Then you can leave that alone and put it on your father's plate.

Edmund puts his knife and fork together. Emma and Laura finish their meal in silence. Emma looks at the children. Laura and Edmund put their hands together

Laura Thank God for my good tea. Thank Father and Mother. Amen.
Edmund Amen.
Emma Amen. (*She gets up and starts to bustle*) Now. We'll keep your father's food warm in the pot so the pig can't have the cooking water yet; but what you can do is help me clear these plates. Come on.

Emma looks back at Laura and Edmund. They are both sitting very glumly

Laura. Edmund. What's the matter?

Laura and Edmund look at each other. Then Laura speaks

Laura Mother. We're sorry if we told lies. Aren't we?
Edmund Yes.
Laura It's just that we didn't think you'd let us go.
Emma Oh, I'd have let you go, Laura. Or I hope I would. I understand that Old Sally wants you to help her.
Laura Yes.
Emma Well, I'm proud of you — but I don't want you to tell me any of Sally's business. That *wouldn't* be right. Understand?
Laura Yes.
Emma That's all right then. I tell you what. Help clear these plates and then have a bit of a read and go to bed with a peppermint each. How's that?
Laura Oh! Can we!

Emma and Laura clear. Edmund sits thinking

Edmund Mother. Are there any witches now?
Emma No. They seem to have all died out. But when I was your age there were plenty of old people who'd known one. Of course, we know there *were* witches because we read about them in the Bible.

Laura and Edmund exchange a glance

What book are you reading now, Laura?
Laura *Gulliver's Travels.*
Emma Oh, that was given me by the Reverend Mr Johnstone, when I was a nursemaid to his children.

Laura Mother, shall we put these flowers on the table for when Father sits down?

Emma That's a *very* good idea, Laura.

Laura (*moving the jar of flowers from the window sill to the table, where Albert's place awaits him*) Mother, is it true you nearly didn't marry Father?

Emma Well, I nearly went to Australia.

Edmund Why didn't you?

Emma I would have gone but somebody told me about the snakes there and I said, "I won't go, for I can't abide the horrid creatures."

Laura Did you know Father already?

Emma No. There was a stonemason needed to work on the church and as you know your father was sent from Oxford.

Edmund When you met him and got married, and lived happily ever after in this end house.

Emma Yes.

Laura He is late again, isn't he?

Edmund He's here, it's him; it's Father!

Emma If you can see when he comes in that he's cross, don't ask him questions.

Edmund glances out into the dusk. The door opens and Albert stands there. He is a little belligerently drunk

Albert. You're late, my dear.

Albert No, I'm not.

Emma We've had our tea. Haven't we, children?

Albert Good. Very good. That means there's room at the table for my friend.

Emma Your friend? What friend?

Albert Come on, friend. Enter, friend.

A tramp comes uneasily in. He is a dirty, unshaven man in rags and a battered bowler

Tramp Good-evening. God bless you, mum. Good-evening.

Emma Albert. He's a tramp.

Tramp That's right.

Albert I found him in a ditch. I heard a noise and looked down, and there he was.

Emma You go upstairs children. You can finish your reading in bed, Laura. Then I'll come up to say Gentle Jesus.

Laura and Edmund go upstairs

Albert Come on, brother. Sit down.
Emma Albert!
Albert Sit yourself down. There's a place laid.
Tramp Thank you. Thank you, brother.
Emma This is no brother of mine.
Albert "Gentle Jesus meek and mild, look upon this little child" — but don't look upon this man in the ditch, is that it?
Emma Albert — he smells.
Tramp I had just such an house as your'n, mum. It burned down in a flood.
Emma (*giving him a half loaf*) Yes, well you take this here.
Tramp Thank you, mum. Thank you.
Emma And now you've got it, go! Go on! Go!
Tramp Thank you, mum! God bless you! God bless you!

He goes

Emma I can't have them in the house, Albert. I can't. When in Rome I must do as the Romans do.
Albert This isn't Rome. It's Lark Rise — the spot God made with left-overs when he'd finished creating the rest of the earth. (*He sits down*)

Silence. Emma gets his tea

I was born on the very day — the very day — of the Battle of the Alma.
Emma I know. I know you were.
Albert We were fighting the Russians. Hard and cruel they were, and thought that might was right but found themselves mistaken. They could not make slaves of a free people.

Silence

Emma Laura and me put the flowers for you.

He is moved. He wants very much to communicate with her and to live in a way that enables him to express his ideals

Albert They're none of them — not one of them — as beautiful as you.

She sits. Silence. They are both moved. Then she decides that since nothing can be changed it is best to be normal and to tell the hamlet news of the day

Emma They took poor Mr Sharman away this morning and, what d'you think, my father managed to walk round.

Albert Did you see old Sharman go?
Emma He took it very hard.
Albert Did they leave him his dignity?
Emma No.

Silence

Albert How are the children? What's Laura's book?
Emma *Gulliver's Travels.*
Albert Good. Good. (*He lifts his head so that Laura upstairs can hear him shout*) Good girl, Laura!

Albert and Emma stare at each other

How are you, my dear? How do you feel?
Emma I feel very well, Albert, considering I'm in my fourth month.

Silence. Emma gets up and looks out of the window

There's young John Price saying goodbye to his Polly.

John Price and Polly are standing in the doorway of her mother's cottage

John Price Don't 'ee fret, Polly. You'll go back to your place tomorrow and in another twelve month you'll be back here, bursting wi' London pride, and a twelvemonth after that we'll be married.

Polly weeps a little. Price holds her. They pass on. Emma turns away from the window

Emma How about you, Albert? How was your work? Are you as tired as you look?
Albert Me? I'm as happy as a lark. Come Michaelmas we'll give notice here and move over to Candleford.

Scene 3

A rumbustious tune from the band sets the scene as Pumpkin, Bishie, Old Price and Boamer settle themselves in the public house, the Waggon and Horses

Landlord The first day of the harvest went well, then?
Pumpkin Went well? We dragged us guts out.
Bishie Good old Boamer lad.
Landlord So they did you proud, Boamer?
Boamer They did. That they did, Landlord. And will tomorrow, until the
work be done with no flinchin'.

Old David makes his entrance

Bishie Here be the oldest inhabitant still workin' and drinkin'.
Old Price Evening, David.
Old David Evening.
Pumpkin I thought you might have brung out your secret savings, Master
Tuffrey, and bought that tea service off the Cheapjack.
Bishie If you had, you could have been like young Mrs Shaw, what was in
very la-di-da service.
Old Price What about Mrs Shaw?
Bishie Ties a blue bow round the handle of her chamber pot.

Laughter

Old David It's when I hear you boys a-talking that I understands why the
old rector preaches agin this place. What did he call it?
Bishie A den of iniquity.
Pumpkin That be it!
Old Price We can't afford more than one half-pint of a night, and he calls
it a den of iniquity.

Laughter

Bishie Ask me, 'tis a great pity he can't come and see what it's like for his
own self.
Old Price Pity he can't mind his own business.

In the end house, Emma prays with the children

Emma ⎫   Gentle Jesus, meek and mild,
Laura ⎬ (*together*)   Look upon this little child,
Edmund ⎭   Pity my simplicity
                                      And suffer me to come to thee.
Old David Well, 'tis his business, come to think on't. The man's paid to
preach, mind, and he's got to find summat to preach against, stands to
reason.

Back in the pub, Albert makes his entrance

Bishie Evening, Mr Timms.
Albert Evening.
Old David Evening.
Old Price We was just a-talking about the old rector.
Albert Don't the women say that his chief virtue is that when he visits them at home he never talks about religion?
Bishie Can't leave much else, can it?
Old David Him's a gentleman born, though.
Old Price He is. He's no counter-jumper.
Albert He's no right to talk politics from the pulpit — which he does, and has done ever since they gave householders the vote.
Pumpkin Well spoke, Mr Timms. I worked away in Northampton and I be radical.
Landlord I'm a true blue, Pumpkin, so mind your sentiments.

Women outside are listening

Mrs Peverill Here it be! Politics! Now you listen!
Pumpkin Joseph Arch is my sentiments, Landlord. Joseph Arch is the man for the farm labourers and I'm proud to have a-shook his hand.
Landlord If I was in Downing Street I'd not give house room to Joseph Arch, nor his trades union.
Bishie What does it matter who's in Downing Street? Whoever 'tis they won't give us nothin', and they can't take nothin' away from us, for you can't get blood out of a stone.
Pumpkin That's not you talking is it, Bishie?
Boamer Oh, he's up on the roof one minute and down the well the next.
Bishie What's having the vote done for us? Tell me that?
Old David First time I had a vote, Squire Bracewell drove me in his carriage. But I voted Liberal! He! He!
Boamer I should hope you did, Father.
Old David They took the poor old hoss to the water but he didn't drink out of their trough! Not he!
Albert I call that a bit low down, to roll up in anybody's carriage to vote against 'em.
Old David Low down? It were rainin'!
Old Price Ask me, David, we gets ten bob a week and we earns every penny on it; but we doesn't earn no more; we takes hemmed good care o' that!

Laughter

Albert What does that show, Master Price?
Old Price What do it show? It shows us knows us own mind. We don't live
in no threepence a week tied housen, 'cause it stands to reason that them
as does allus got to do just what they be told, or out they goes.
Old David Neck and crop.
Old Price Bag and baggage. But us can't be told 'cause us pay a shillin' a
week to live in the Rise.
Albert That didn't save old Sharman, did it?
Old Price It saved him afore he got feeble!

The women outside have been eagerly following

Mrs Peverill There! See? The old cocks don't like it when the young cocks
start to crow.
Landlord Say as you will, it's no good you chaps thinking you're goin'
against the gentry.
Mrs Blaby Just what I says! If the men have to vote why don't they vote Tory
and keep in with the gentry?
Mrs Peverill You don't never hear of Liberals giving the poor a bit o' coal
or a blanket at Christmas, do you?
Mrs Blaby O' course not. O' course we don't.
Landlord They've got the land and they've got the money *and* they'll keep
it. Where'd you be without them to give you work and pay your wages, I'd
like to know.
Albert (*deciding that the moment to speak has come*) Where we'd be,
Landlord, is where we are now — all on us a-voting for Mr Gladstone, who
can change things and make 'em better.

The men heartily agree, even the old ones

Old David Well, I never thought I'd agree that much with 'ee, Mr Timms!
Boamer Come on, lads: "People's William".

They all burst into the song "The People's William"

Song

Band   God bless the people's William
                          Long may he lead the van
                          Of Liberty and freedom
                          God bless the Grand Old Man.

*The men heartily applaud themselves. The Landlord decides to change the
subject*

Landlord How's about a bit of song from you, Algy? Just to oblige?

Algy is tall, thin and getting old, a weedy stooping creature with watery-blue eyes and long ginger side-whiskers. His voice is high and a bit cracked but there is something about him of both a military bearing and a man of culture

Algy Oh, bai Jove, I say, Landlord, I mean dash it all, bai Jove ...
Albert I hear they've put him on half pay.
Landlord Well: what can he do except work with the women?
Pumpkin Come on, Algy. Wert up!
Algy When I ... when I was in the Grenadier Guards ...
Boamer Where does he come from? That's what I'd like to know.
Old Price Knocked at the door of an house, didn't he?
Old David Twenty year ago.
Old Price At midnight. In a thunderstorm.
Pumpkin Remember what he did when the German band came?
Bishie German band, Algy.
Algy Bai Jove. What?
Pumpkin German band's a-comin!

The group oomph-oompah like the German band that visits the hamlet once a year. Algy sticks his fingers in his ears and howls. The music stops. Algy looks bewildered

Albert Joking, Algy. Only joking.
Algy Bai Jove ...
Bishie What about that song, then?
Algy To oblige, what? Same as usual? Ready! Steady! Go!

Algy sings "Have You Ever Been in the Peninsula?"

Song

> Have you ever been in the Peninsula?
> If not I advise you to stay where you are
> For should you adore a
> Sweet Spanish senor-ah
> She may prove what some might call sin-gu-lah

The men clap politely while Algy returns to his seat

Cockie and Master Pridham enter the pub

Boamer Evening, Cockie.
Bishie Master Pridham.

At the end house, Emma looks at the children to see if they are asleep. Laura is not

Laura Mother ...
Emma Shhhh ... Go back to sleep.
Laura Where's Father?
Emma He's just walked out a while.
Laura Will you walk out?
Emma I might go and sit at the door with Queenie.
Laura Tell me a story.
Emma No, Laura. Edmund's asleep.
Laura Something out of your own head.
Emma Well, first you lie down again. Once upon a time, there was a little girl and when she wasn't out for mushrooms she was out for berries, on a heath just like the Hardwick Heath, where we went blackberrying, you know, and when she looked down under one bush she saw a little wooden door in the ground. She opened the door and there were some steps and she went down the steps and what d'you think? They led to an underground palace where everything was blue and silver. Silver tables and silver chairs and silver plates to eat off and all the cushions and curtains were made of pale blue satin ...

In the pub, the Landlord calls on Chad Gubbins to dance

Landlord Come on, Chad. Do your bit. Paid on in ale!

Chad Gubbins,who is a morris dancer, gets up and does a dance. He uses Bishie's hat as a marker and at the end of the dance he jumps on it and returns it to Bishie amid applause from the men

Pumpkin What's old Master Price up to in his corner over there? Ain't heard him strike up tonight.
Bishie He only knows his old "Outlandish Knight".
Boamer Poor old feller be eighty-three. Let 'un sing while he can.

Old Price rises and announces "Outlandish Knight"

Old Price   An outlandish knight from the Northlands came,
                         And he came a-wooing of me.

Mrs Peverill They'll soon be out now. There's poor Old Price a-singing of his "Outlandish Knight".

Old Price　　　And he told me he'd take me up to the Northlands
　　　　　　　　And there he would marry me.

　　　　　　　　Go fetch me some of your father's gold,
　　　　　　　　And some of your mother's tea,
　　　　　　　　And the two finest horses from your father's stables,
　　　　　　　　Where they stand thirty and three.

　　　　　　　　He's mounted him up on his milk white steed,
　　　　　　　　She's rode on the dapple grey,
　　　　　　　　And they rode till they came to the broad sea-short,
　　　　　　　　Three hours before it was day.

　　　　　　　　Light down, light down from your horse, he cries,
　　　　　　　　And deliver it over to me,
　　　　　　　　For six pretty maids I have drowned here,
　　　　　　　　And the seventh one you'll surely be.

　　　　　　　　Take off, take off your silken gown,
　　　　　　　　And deliver it unto me,
　　　　　　　　For I think it's not fitting so costly a robe,
　　　　　　　　Should all rot away in the sea.

　　　　　　　　Light down, light down off your horse, she cries,
　　　　　　　　And turn your back to me,
　　　　　　　　I think it's not fitting a fine gentleman
　　　　　　　　A naked lady should see.

　　　　　　　　He's lighted him down from his lily white steed,
　　　　　　　　And turned his back to she,
　　　　　　　　And she's catched him round his middle so small,
　　　　　　　　And threw the old sod in the sea.

Landlord Anthem lads. Wert up, Master Pridham. Let's be having of my favourite — Pratty Flowers.

Master Pridham and the men sing "Abroad for Pleasure"

Song

Pridham	Abroad for pleasure as I was a walking,
	'Twas on a summer, summer calm and clear.
All	Abroad for pleasure as I was a walking,
	'Twas on a summer, summer calm and clear.
Pridham	There I beheld the most beautiful damsel,
	Lamenting for her shepherd swain.
All	There I beheld the most beautiful damsel,
	Lamenting for her shepherd swain,
	Lamenting for her shepherd swain.
Pridham	Wilt thou go fight the French and Spaniards,
	Wilt thou leave me thus my dear.
All	Wilt thou go fight the French and Spaniards,
	Wilt thou leave me thus my dear,
	Wilt thou leave me thus my dear.
Pridham	No more to yon green banks will I take me.
	With pleasure for to rest myself and view the lambs.
All	No more to yon green banks will I take me.
	With pleasure for to rest myself and view the lambs.
Pridham	But I will take me to yon green gardens.
	Where the pratty flowers grow.
All	But I will take me to yon green gardens.
	Where the pratty flowers grow,
	Where the pratty, pratty flowers grow.

Applause as the song ends and then it is closing time

Landlord You'll be leading them again tomorrow, Boamer?
Boamer That I will, for I'm the King of the Mowers.
Pumpkin Good-night, Master Price.
Old Price Good-night, Pumpkin.
Algy Bai Jove ... What?
Bishie Don't you be forgetting your bedtime cup of soapsuds, Master Price.
Old Price Them cleans the outers, Bishie, so it stands to reason they clean the innards too.

They have all left now except Albert and Boamer who stand and shake hands

Albert Well. Good-night, Boamer. Soon be harvest home.
Boamer Ay. It will. Soon be the Old Queen's Jubilee an' all.

The band now plays the hymn tune as the actors reset the benches and the space becomes the church

SCENE 4

The actors process into church and the Rector goes up to the first level. They then stand and sing "The Day Thou Gavest, Lord, is Ended"

Hymn

All   The day thou gavest, Lord, is ended,
              The darkness falls at thy behest;
              To thee our morning hymns ascended,
              Thy praise shall sanctify our rest.

During the second verse Laura and Edmund walk to the back of the church

              So be it, Lord, thy throne shall never,
              Like earth's proud empires, pass away;
              Thy kingdom stands, and grows for ever,
              Till all thy creatures own thy sway.

Laura After the Jubilee, nothing ever seemed quite the same. The old rector died and the farmer retired and machines put people out of work. Early in the nineties some measure of relief came, for then the weekly wage was raised to fifteen shillings; but rising prices and new requirements soon absorbed this rise, and it took a world war to obtain anything like a living wage.

A harmonica plays a fragment of the tune "The Battle of the Somme"

Rector To the glory of God, in memory of those from this parish whose lives have been given in defence of their country and in the cause of right and justice in the Great War, 1914 to 1918 AD: J. Blaby, W. Blaby, E.A.V. Blencowe, A.D. Cross, H. Farrer, S. Gaskin, H. Harris, E. Peverill, W. Peverill, E. Timms.
Edmund E. Timms? That's me!
Laura Hush, Edmund!
Rector Their names liveth for evermore.

The band crashes into "The Battle of the Somme" as the actors line up for the final photo pose. They disperse with the music and this is the end of the

play itself. But then the Leader of the band calls for a Grand Circle Dance
and the cast form up and do the dance. Then members of the audience are
invited to join in, and the whole process is repeated

Band Leader Thank you. Good-night.

Black-out

FURNITURE AND PROPERTY LIST

ACT I
SCENE 1

On stage: Table. *On it*: plate with piece of bread, apron, tools, billycock hat
Chairs
Flower jar
Mats
Brush
Rug beater
Packed dinner basket

Personal: **Mr Morris**: ash stick
Men: scythes

SCENE 2

Set: Knives, forks, plates of mushrooms on table
Rugs and beaters for **Women**
Hoop for **Laura**

SCENE 3

Set: Sprig of rosemary

SCENE 4

Set: Chair and coat for **Major**

Personal: **Old Postie**: postbag containing letters and small parcels

SCENE 5

Off stage: Bunch of freshly cut flowers (**Grandfather**)

Personal: **Twister**: open clasp knife
Emma: handkerchief

SCENE 6

Off stage: Cart with fish, fruit and bell (**Jerry**)

ACT II
SCENE 1

Set: Pitchfork
Iron spoon

Personal: **Queenie**: snuffbox

SCENE 2

Personal: **Mrs Beamish**: saucer

SCENE 3

Off stage: Gun, haversack, brace of dead rabbits (**Squire Bracewell**)

SCENE 4

Personal: **Men**: clasp knives, food wrapped in handkerchiefs, jug of ale, clay pipes,
tobacco
Boamer: stick, string
Old Price: watch

ACT III
SCENE 1

Set: Sewing, novelettes for **Women**

SCENE 2

Set: Stone for **Edmund**

ACT IV
SCENE 1

Off stage: Cart of crockery and tinware, naptha flare (practical), matches
(**Cheapjack**)

Personal: **Price**: money

SCENE 2

Set: Knives and forks, loaf of bread, plates on food on table
             Jar of flowers

SCENE 3

Set: Benches
             Glasses of beer

SCENE 4

Re-set: Benches

LIGHTING PLOT

Property fittings required: nil

Various interior and exterior settings

To open: Bring up general lighting on Band

Cue 1:	**Laura** and **Edmund** go	(Page 2)
	Change to pearly pink dawn effect	

ACT I. Morning

To open: Morning summer sunshine effect

No cues

ACT II. Midday

To open: Midday summer sunshine effect

No cues

ACT III. Afternoon

To open: Afternoon summer sunshine effect

No cues

ACT IV. Evening

To open: Summer evening effect, gradually becoming dusk

Cue 2	**Band Leader**: "Thank you. Good-night."	(Page 58)
	Black-out	

CANDLEFORD

CHARACTERS

Laura, 14
Edmund, 12
Emma Timms
Albert Timms

Mrs Peverill
Mrs Andrews
Landlord

Dorcas Lane
Zillah, her maid
Matthew, the foreman
Bill
Bavour   } apprentice smiths
Solomon

Thomas Brown, the postman
Mrs Gubbins
Mrs Macey

John
Robert

Mr Chitty
Sir Timothy, the squire
Sir Austin
Mrs Gascoigne
Mr Rowbotham
Lavinia
Lavinia's mother
Lavinia's fiancé
Huntsman

Cinderella Doe
Loony Joe
Cowman Jolliffe

Mr Coulsdon, the rector
Mr Wilkins, the carrier
Minnie Hickman, the telegram girl
Ben Trollope ⎱ old soldiers
Tom Ashley ⎰
Mr Cochrane, the Post Office Inspector
John, Laura's husband

CANDLEFORD

Commissioned by the National Theatre and first presented at the Cottesloe
Theatre on 14th November 1979, with the following cast:

Edmund	Benedict Beddard or Paul Davies-Prowles
Matthew	J. G. Devlin
Zillah	Edna Dore
Cowman Jolliffe, Mr Coulsdon	Howard Goorney
Sir Timothy	Gawn Grainger
Albert Timms, Mr Wilkins, Tom Ashley	James Grant
Ben Trollope, Loony Joe	Tony Haygarth
John, Mr Cochrane	Dave Hill
Dorcas Lane	Morag Hood
Minnie	Louisa Livingstone
Bavour	Kevin McNally
Emma Timms, Mrs Macey	Mary Miller
Mrs Gubbins, Cinderella Doe	Peggy Mount
Thomas Brown	Bill Owen
Robert, John	Brian Protheroe
Bill	John Salthouse
Solomon	John Tams
Laura	Valerie Whittington

Directed by Bill Bryden and Sebastian Graham-Jones
Designed by William Dudley
Musical Directors, Ashley Hutchings and John Tams
Music by the Albion Band

CANDLEFORD

The band plays an overture to welcome the audience. Cinderella Doe and Loony Joe mix amongst the people telling fortunes during the last thirty seconds. Laura is standing near, and at the end of the overture Cinderella tells Laura's fortune

Cinderella Doe Tell your fortune, missy? What's your name?
Laura Laura.
Cinderella Laura, your future's pleasing, Laura. There is no fair man or dark man or enemy to beware of in it.
Laura Can you promise me love?
Cinderella Love? Laura, you're going to be loved by people you've never seen and never will see. Sometimes we see things we don't understand, Laura.

The Lights fade. The band plays the first choruses of "The Year Turns Round"

Song

Band   Cruel winter cuts through like the reaper
The old year lies withered and slain,
But like Barleycorn who rose from the grave
A new year will rise up again.

Chorus   And the snow falls
And the wind calls
And the year turns round again.

I'll wager a hatful of guineas
Against all the songs you can sing
That some day you'll love and the next day you'll lose
And winter will turn into spring.

The Lights come up on the actors in a photo pose

Chorus   And the snow falls
And the wind calls

> And the year turns round again.

After the second chorus the actors disperse, leaving the Timms family group; Laura, Edmund, Emma and Albert. It is before dawn

Laura wears a grey cashmere frock with a white lace collar and leg of mutton sleeves. Her pigtail has been looped up and tied once with a big black ribbon at the back of her neck

Laura One day when Laura was thirteen a letter came from Candleford Green. It said that Miss Dorcas Lane wanted a learner for her post office work, and thought Laura would do, if her parents were willing; which they were. There were now four younger children to be provided for in the little cottage at Lark Rise, and Laura's future must depend upon herself and what opportunities might offer.

Band   But there will come a time of great plenty,
                A time of good harvest and sun
                Until then put your trust in tomorrow my friend
                For yesterday's over and done.

Chorus   And the snow falls
                And the wind calls
                And the year turns round again.

Albert Well, I'd best put your trunk in the spring-cart.
Emma Ay. Laura, mind you sponge and press that ribbon for it cost good money. And when you come to buy your own clothes ...
Edmund Mother, how far is Candleford Green?
Emma Eight miles, Edmund. Go help your father.

Edmund goes. Mother and daughter are alone

> Like I say — always buy the best you can afford. It pays in the end.
Laura Mother: if I make mistakes in the post office I'll not be thought stupid, will I?
Emma God bless the child. Always looking for trouble. Just be your own natural self and Dorcas, I'm sure, will be hers.
Laura What should I call her? Should I "Cousin Dorcas" her?
Emma Come to that, perhaps you'd better not. It'd better be Miss Lane. You'll get on like an house on fire.
Laura My hair is all right, isn't it?
Emma It's how we saw that girl behind the post office counter at Sherston wear hers, isn't it?

Laura She had a coloured ribbon.
Emma Coloured ribbons make girls look like horses at a fair.

Laura smiles. Then Emma unburdens herself

I've thought all day about when you were born, Laura. It was such deep snow. The doctor had to walk the last mile and when you put in your appearance he said "There you are, there is the person who has caused all this pother. Let us hope she will prove worth it!" And when my father saw you he — You do think about him, don't you, Laura? You're the only one I can talk to about him. Your father and he never got on together and the others were too young when he died to remember him. Lots of things happened before they were born that you'll always remember, so I shall always have someone to talk to about the old times.

Silence. They do not need to speak. Then Albert and Edmund return

Albert All set, my dear. The old pony can't wait to be off.

People appear from one cottage and another to say goodbye

Emma Ay. Then we'd best say goodbye, Laura. Goodbye.

They embrace

(*Stepping back*) Goodbye. Don't forget to write to me.
Edmund And to me, and address it to my very own self!

Laura gets into the cart. Albert is beside her

Mrs Peverill Goodbye, Laura. Mind you be a good girl now and does just as you be told.
Mrs Andrews Pleasant journey, Laura. Hope you'll have a good place.
Landlord Wrap every penny stamp up in a smile!

Laura smiles. She sniffs back a tear. Albert watches her and then squeezes her hand

Albert Ay. Lark Rise is your home, such as it is. I suppose.

They continue their journey, the band plays "Music for Laura's Journey"

When the music ends we are at Candleford Green, six months later, before the first light on a mid-winter morning. It is bitterly cold

The Journeymen have just got up

Solomon By hem. I never knowed nothing like that garden privy. Coldest
  place I ever set foot in.
Bavour Tell you what might warm us all up.
Solomon What?
Bavour If you was to help young Bill here with the forge.

They box

Bill Wert up. It's Bob Fitzsimmons.

The smiths sing "The Holly and the Ivy" (Coventry Version)

Song

Smiths The holly and the ivy
  When they are both full grown
  Of all the trees that are in the green wood
  The holly bears the crown.

  The rising of the sun
  And running of the deer,
  The playing of the merry organ,
  Sweet singing in the choir.

  The holly bears a prickle
  Sharp as any thorn
  And Mary bore sweet Jesus Christ
  On Christmas day in the morn.

Matthew, the foreman, joins them

Matthew Bavour, you're not eating again, are you?
Bavour I like a bit o' summat to peck at between meals, Matthew.
Matthew Between meals? You've just this instant come from your
  breakfast.

*One of the smiths' tricks is tossing conversation to each other as though it was
an anthem in church*

Bill (*singing*) Oh, Solomon, can you please give us an hand and pump them
  bellows?

Solomon (*singing*) Oh, Bill, the bellows is just a-coming up!
Matthew I know why Bavour never sings: 'cause the bugger's allus eating.

Bill lights the shavings. Solomon pumps. The forge fire flares and grows

Bill There she goes.

In the house Laura comes downstairs. She has a storm lantern, and Dorcas Lane and Zillah carry an oil lamp as they come from the kitchen to the living-room

Laura Morning, Miss Lane. Morning, Zillah.
Dorcas Morning Laura.
Zillah Morning.

Dorcas is dark, erect, bright-eyed and dressed in silk with a satin apron embroidered in jet. Her hair is plaited into a coronet above a fringe. She sits down with a cup of tea. Zillah the maid is greying with bad feet and rheumatism. She starts to clear up after the men's breakfast

Laura Laura lived with Miss Lane and Zillah and the men, who slept on featherbeds in the attic, in a long low white house which might have been taken for an ordinary cottage of the more substantial kind but for the painted board which read CANDLEFORD GREEN POST AND TELE-GRAPH OFFICE. At the other end of the building was another board, which read DORCAS LANE SHOEING AND GENERAL SMITH. Inside, the house clock was always set half an hour fast, so that when Laura got up at seven to sort the morning post, it was really only half-past six.

Laura takes her lamp to the post office and hangs it up. She lights the oilstove. Mrs Gubbins, the older of the two women letter-sorters, comes up the lane past the Smithy. She is crabbed and uncouth

Matthew Morning, Mrs Gubbins.
Bavour Morning.
Mrs Gubbins (*her answer is a grunt*) Huh!
Bavour Ask me, that Mrs Gubbins is a grumpy old sow, like.
Matthew A boychap like you oughter have more respect than utter a thought like that: even if it is true.

Mrs Gubbins enters the post office

Laura Morning, Mrs Gubbins.

Mrs Gubbins Huh!

Solomon Ay. It's a-cause she's an ancient widow-woman.

Matthew By hem, boy, you really be as wise as Solomon.

Bill (*singing to tune of "O Come all ye Faithful"*) That's why you give him Solomon for a nickname, ain't it?

Matthew Oh come on. It's hunt morning and nothing done yet.

Postman Brown comes up the lane singing

Brown   Deep and wide, deep and wide,
            There's a fountain flowing deep and wide.
            Hallelujah for it.
            Deep and wide, deep and wide,
            There's a fountain flowing deep and wide.

Solomon Here it is, lads! Old Salvation himself!

Bavour Morning, Mr Brown.

Brown Morning, young Bavour.

Matthew Morning, Thomas.

Brown Morning, Matthew.

Bill You're late, aren't you, Mr Brown?

Brown So would you be if you'd a-walked from Candleford in this weather: there's some of them snowdrifts half blocks the road. (*Singing*) "Deep and wide ..."

Smiths (*joining in with last lines of song*) "There's a fountain flowing that is *very* ..." (*continue with actions only*)

Matthew Come inside.

Brown enters the post office

Laura Morning, Mr Brown.

Brown How is it with your soul, young Laura?

Laura Well, I just wish I didn't have to wear these mittens.

Brown What about you, Mrs Gubbins? Have you found salvation?

Mrs Gubbins Huh?

Brown Have you found salvation?

Mrs Gubbins Not since last evening's delivery I haven't, no.

Brown I'll pray for you. I'll speak to Jesus.

Mrs Gubbins Ay. Just ax him about this here weather.

Brown Weather? No use axin' about weather. Weather's sent a-purpose to torment postmen.

Silence. They all work

Mrs Gubbins Zillah!

Zillah Ay, what is it?

Mrs Gubbins Where's that cup o' tea?

Zillah I'm still a-clearing up the men's breakfast.

Brown All right for the men, b'ain't it? Stood round that old forge all day.

Laura It's hard work for them today, Mr Brown — with the Hunt Meeting and all.

Brown Ay. Allus the same. First Saturday in January. For twenty year it's been weather to try a saint.

Silence. They work. Mrs Macey the younger woman letter-carrier crosses the Green from her cottage

Matthew Morning, Mrs Macey.

Mrs Macey Good-morning, Matthew. (*She wears an old tippet against the cold, a long grey ulster coat and a man's bowler hat draped with a veil. She is delicate and refined. She was born in the country but lived for a while in London. She enters the post office*). Good-morning.

Brown Morning.

Laura Morning, Mrs Macey.

Mrs Macey Morning, Laura. Mrs Gubbins.

Mrs Gubbins Humph!

Mrs Macey What weather! What huge snowdrifts! (*She sets to work at the sorting*) It makes me envy my husband, I must say. He's travelling abroad, you know, and his gentleman's not ready to come home. I expect that while we're carrying the mail they're out shooting tigers.

Mrs Gubbins In Spain.

Mrs Macey What?

Mrs Gubbins You said last week he was in Spain.

Mrs Macey Oh. Er — Yes. He is.

Brown Well I'll be jiggered. If it ain't the same as every other bad morning. There's a letter for every house on my delivery even them as don't have one once in a blue moon.

Mrs Gubbins It's done a-purpose, ain't it?

Brown That don't stop me bein' jiggered, Mrs Gubbins.

Mrs Gubbins Huh!

Laura There's one here for you, Mrs Macey.

Mrs Macey Oh. Thank you.

Laura gives Mrs Macey the letter. Mrs Macey opens and reads it. Brown has returned to sorting. The first letter he touches proves his point

Brown Here. What did I tell 'ee? Here's one from that chap in Australia what don't write but once in a twelvemonth.

Mrs Macey (*a cry of distress*) Oh ...!
Laura Not bad news, I hope, Mrs Macey?
Mrs Macey I must go. I must go at once.
Brown Go?
Mrs Macey Now. Immediately.
Brown You can't leave your letters half-sorted.
Mrs Macey I must.
Brown What about your delivery?
Mrs Macey No. No, I have to go.
Laura Should I call Miss Lane?
Mrs Macey No. Don't call her here, please. I must see her alone and in
  private. And I shan't be able to take out the letters this morning. Oh dear!
  Oh dear! What's to be done?
Laura (*leading the way from the post office to the living-room*) Miss Lane!
  Excuse me, Miss Lane!
Dorcas What is it?
Laura Mrs Macey.
Dorcas What about her?

Mrs Macey holds out the letter. Dorcas takes it and glances at it

  Humph! Come in. Have some tea. Then tell me all about it. (*To Laura*) Tell
  Zillah not to begin cooking breakfast until I tell her to.
Laura Yes, Miss Lane.
Dorcas (*afterthought*) Say she is to go upstairs and begin getting my room
  ready for turning out.
Laura Yes, Miss Lane.

*Dorcas and Mrs Macey go into the living-room. Zillah has heard the
commotion and arrives bursting with curiosity*

Zillah What is it? Eh? Oh, I say! What carryings on!
Laura Miss Lane says not to cook breakfast until she tells you and will you
  go upstairs and turn out her room?
Zillah Eh?
Laura Will you go upstairs and ...
Zillah I heard. I heard. And I know what it allus means. It means go upstairs
  so as you can't dratted well listen at keyholes!

*Mrs Macey sobs. Zillah goes, highly indignant. Laura returns to the post
office. Brown and Mrs Gubbins stare at her*

Brown Well? What is it? Eh?

Laura What's what?
Brown Mrs Macey.
Laura I didn't think it was my place to ask.

Brown sighs. Thwarted. Mrs Gubbins chuckles grimly

Mrs Gubbins Just what I allus says. Ax no questions and you'll be told no lies, although you may hear a few without axing.
Brown Though I says it myself, I'm not nosy. Not me. Not like some. I was just asking about a fellow creature.

Silence. Brown's bag is ready but he makes no move to go out on his delivery. Mrs Macey sobs. Laura works. Mrs Gubbins stares at Brown. Then she speaks

Mrs Gubbins What time be it, young Laura?
Laura House clock or Post Office?
Brown Eh?
Mrs Gubbins I'm just-a-thinking: if a delivery do go out late, there's a report put in, ain't there?
Brown Er — Ay. Like I was saying: I'll be on my way. I'll be jiggered if I won't.

More sobs from Mrs Macey. Brown picks up his bag and goes out on his delivery: his round is the village

Brown (*singing*) Deep and wide ...
Mrs Gubbins See? He'd have stayed to overhear what's happened to Mrs Macey but for the fac' that he's already had one report put in against him.
Laura Has he?
Mrs Gubbins Course he has. Over the Sunday delivery.
Laura Oh.
Mrs Gubbins Won't do it, will 'un, not since his conversion? Now — I must start *my* delivery, eh? (*She stops in her tracks*) Fancy that! I can't! I've lost that old piece of string to tie my bag!
Mrs Macey (*entering from the living-room to put her coat on*) Oh yes, of course I must.

Mrs Gubbins pretends to hunt for the string. Laura gathers together Mrs Macey's delivery. Mrs Macey is ready to leave. At the front door of the cottage Dorcas says goodbye to Mrs Macey

Dorcas Are you utterly sure that you wish to take your son with you?

Mrs Macey Yes.
Dorcas He can spend the time with us.
Mrs Macey No. Thank you. I must take him.

They embrace

Oh — perhaps Laura would go over and feed the cat? I'll pay for his milk
when I get back. Tell her whatever you think fit. She's a sensible little soul.
Dorcas Don't worry. I'll see to everything.

*Mrs Macey goes. Dorcas turns inside again. In the post office Mrs Gubbins
whistles to the string as though it was a dog or cat*

Mrs Gubbins String! Come on string!
Dorcas (*entering the post office*) What? Not out yet, Mrs Gubbins?
Mrs Gubbins Can't find my old string, Miss Lane.
Dorcas It's sticking out of your bodice.
Mrs Gubbins By hem! I can't think how it got there!

*Mrs Gubbins snatches at the string and, grumbling to herself, ties up the bag
and goes out on her delivery. When she has gone, Dorcas speaks again*

Dorcas Here's a pretty kettle of fish! We're in a bit of a fix, Laura. Mrs Macey
won't be able to do her round this morning. She's got to go off at once by
train to see her husband, who's dangerously ill. She's gone home to get
ready.
Laura But I thought her husband was abroad.
Dorcas So he may have been at one time, but he isn't now. He's in Reading,
and it'll take her all day to get there and back and a cold miserable journey
it'll be for the poor soul. But I'll tell you more about that later. The thing
now is what are we going to do about the letters and Sir Timothy's private
post-bag? Zillah shan't go. I won't demean myself to ask her, after the
disgraceful way she's been banging about upstairs, not to mention her bad
feet and her rheumatism. And Minnie's got a bad cold. As you know she
couldn't take out the telegrams yesterday. And nobody can be spared from
the forge with this frost and horses pouring in to be rough shod, not to
mention the Hunt this morning; and every moment it's getting later and you
know what old Farmer Stebbing is: if his letters are ten minutes late he
writes to the Postmaster General, though to be sure, he might make some
allowance this morning for snow and late mails. What a fool I must have
been to take on this office. It's nothing but worry, worry, worry.
Laura I suppose I couldn't be spared to go.
Dorcas Oh, *would* you? And you don't think your mother would mind? Well
that's a weight off my mind! Have you sorted the letters?

Laura Yes.

Dorcas What are these?

Laura To be called for at the post office.

Dorcas (*looking at the letters*) Humph! Mr John Gaskin and Mr Robert Bowler.

Laura Aren't they the young footmen at the Hall?

Dorcas They are.

Laura Should I put the letters in Sir Timothy's private bag?

Dorcas No you should not. You should strictly observe the official rules. To be called for at the post office.

Laura seems about to speak but checks herself

If you were about to say that Mrs Macey carries such letters to the Hall my reply is that I am not aware of it, and if I were I would not condone the breaking of the rules. Neither should these impertinent young men expect me to. Now. You're not going out without some breakfast inside you, time or no time, for all the farmers and squires in creation. Zillah! Zillah! Laura's breakfast at once! Bacon and eggs and make haste, please! (*She turns to Laura again*) What is more, it may be Mrs Macey's delivery, but I shall lend you *my* sealskin cap!

As Laura sets out the band plays "The Postman's Knock Song"

Song

Band   Every morning true as the clock
                            Somebody hears the postman's knock
                            Every morning true as the clock
                            Somebody hears the postman's knock

                            So out in the snow young Laura does go
                            And she hastens from door to door.
                            What a medley of news her hands do hold
                            For high, low, rich and poor.
                            In many's the face the joy she can trace
                            In many's the grief she can see
                            As the door opens up to her loud tat-tat
                            And her quick delivery.

Repeat first verse

*At the hall the footmen John and Robert have seen Laura coming and nip out
to meet her*

John Whoa-up then! You ain't the post, are you?
Laura Yes.
John Where's Mrs Macey?
Laura She weren't able to come.
Robert Hey — did us get letters today? Name of Mr Bowler and J. Gaskin,
Esq.
Laura Yes.
John Did you bring 'em?
Laura The post's in the private bag.
John Course it is; and the bag's locked, ain't it, and master has the key and
since he's gone off hunting he won't open 'un till dark. But what us objects
to is not that, as Mrs Macey knows.
Robert That she does.
John What us objects to is when two days arter they was delivered Sir
Timothy does hand over us letters he reads the handwriting and postmarks,
see? And when he don't like 'em, he tells us off.
Robert (*imitating Sir Timothy*) What's this, my young man? Not betting tips
again, is it?
John Course, it's all right for Sir Timothy to have *his* bet.
Robert Course it is.
John But when we have ours we're called young wastrels, ain't we? That's
what us objects to.
Laura I'm sorry.

Silence

I don't think you should be treated like children. I'm sorry.
Robert Somehow, I don't think she has brought us letters. Have you?
Laura No.
Robert Why not?
Laura They have to be collected.
John Course they mun be collected. We know that. So do Mrs Macey.
Laura I'm sorry. I — (*her nerve wobbles*) I forgot.
Robert Oh, come you on. It's perishin' out here.

He starts to walk away. John checks him

John Hold on. Hold on. Will you bring 'em next time?
Laura I might not be here next time.
John But if you is will you bring 'em?

Laura I can't.
John Why not?
Laura It's again official regulations.
John By hem!
Laura I said I'm sorry.
John You said regulations and that means you didn't forget us letters. You did it a-purpose.

Laura is silent. This is her first grown-up problem

John But where's the harm in bringing 'em. Eh? You're not Master's sort. You're ours. Where's the harm?
Laura I signed a Declaration to Her Majesty.
John Declaration! (*He snatches the private bag*)
Laura Give that here.
John Hey!

He throws the bag like a rugby ball to Robert. Laura instinctively chases it

Robert Hey!
Laura I said I'm sorry. I'll ask if I can bring your letters. I will. I promise.
John No use if you has to ask, girl. Same as if you had to ask me for a kiss.

Silence. Then Mr Chitty, the butler shouts out as he comes towards them

Mr Chitty Robert! What are you doing, I'd like to know?
Robert Just fetching the post, Mr Chitty.
Mr Chitty You leave that to me and help Mrs Purchase clean the silver!
John The butler. Give him your private bag.

John gives the bag to Laura. Mr Chitty arrives

Here us comes, Mr Chitty, as ready and willing to do as much for half a crown as us would for a shilling!

John and Robert return to the house. Laura hands Mr Chitty the private bag

Mr Chitty Well, I must say. You look as though you've been drawn through a quickset hedge backwards. Where's Mrs Macey?
Laura She weren't able to come.
Mr Chitty Why not?
Laura Sickness.
Mr Chitty Have they two wastrels been teasing you?

Laura is silent

Don't you worry. Good looks ain't everything, and you can't help it if you
didn't happen to be behind the door when they was being given out.

Laura is doubly silent

As for the rest — well, you're only young once. You must get all the fun
you can. You give young wastrels like them two as good as they give you
and they'll soon learn to respect you. Now, do you want a cup o' tea, or has
this snow made your delivery late?
Laura Yes.
Mr Chitty Then off you go, girl, and do your duty!

The band strikes up again with "Postman's Knock"

Song

Band   Every morning as true as the clock,
                  Somebody hears the postman's knock
                  Every morning as true as the clock
                  Somebody hears the postman's knock.

                  Number one she presents with news of a birth
                  With tidings of death number four
                  At thirteen a bill of terrible length
                  She drops through the hole in the door
                  Now a cheque or an order
                  At fifteen she leaves
                  At sixteen her presence doth prove
                  And seventeen doth an acknowledgement get
                  And eighteen a letter of love.

                  Every morning as true as the clock,
                  Somebody hears the postman's knock
                  Every morning as true as the clock
                  Somebody hears the postman's knock.

*At Candleford Green it is nearly ten o'clock. Dorcas keeps the telegraph
machine in the living-room, under a sort of tea-cosy. She whips off the cosy.
Zillah stands on a chair so that she can reach the post office clock*

Dorcas Zillah! Are you ready, Zillah?
Zillah I'm on the old chair all right, Miss Lane.
Dorcas The telegraph's late by this clock.
Zillah Ay. Us is all fast again! Ask me it's a-cause ...
Dorcas Sssh! ...

They wait. Silence. Then the telegraph bell rings

Dorcas Hah!
Zillah Oh!
Dorcas Ssh!

The machine starts to clatter. Miss Lane reads the dial

It is ten o'clock — *now*!
Zillah Now!
Dorcas How fast was the post office?
Zillah Half a minute, Miss Lane.
Dorcas I don't know how we'd keep straight without these daily time checks.

In the forge Matthew lectures the smiths. Laura walks up past them

Matthew Now, you lads. It's ten o'clock and I just a-putting on my second-
  best coat for the hunt. I'm expecting you to get on with your work. None
  of that gaping and gazing. You've seen horses afore, and them that ride
  'em: though to judge by some of your doings I'd think you didn't know
  their near from their off sides. Is my meaning clear?
Solomon It is, Matthew.
Bill Ay.
Bavour Ay.
Matthew Then look to it!
Laura *(hearing the horn blowing)* It's the hunt.
Zillah Miss Dorcas, there they be!
Dorcas We'll observe them from upstairs.

The Hunt enters, magnificent, to music. They pull up on the Green

Sir Timothy Morning, Miss Lane.
Dorcas Morning, Sir Timothy.
Mrs Gascoine Morning, Timothy.
Sir Timothy Morning, Mrs Gascoine. Morning, Austin.
Sir Austin Morning.
Bill There's Loony Joe a-gaping at the hounds.

Loony Joe is making noises at the dogs

Sir Timothy Morning, Matthew.
Matthew Morning, Sir Timothy. How's that fetlock?
Sir Timothy You couldn't take a look, could you?
Matthew I certainly could, sir.
Sir Timothy That chap's the best horse doctor in three counties.
Sir Austin Really?
Sir Timothy Absolutely. Amazing man. Morning, my lord. Your health, Mr
  Rowbotham.
Mr Rowbotham And yours, Sir Timothy.
Sir Timothy Good-morning. Morning, Lavinia.
Lavinia Good-morning.

Loony Joe makes noises

Huntsman Hi Spot. Hi there.
Bill It's all right, Huntsman. He's just a harmless loony.
Huntsman Just so long as he don't think he's one of 'em.
Laura Oh, Miss Lane. What a sight it is!
Dorcas It is, if you don't look too closely.
Laura How's that?
Dorcas That gentleman there.
Zillah Where?
Dorcas There.

Laughter from Sir Austin and Mrs Gascoine

That's Sir Austin on the tall grey. He's out-running the constable, I'm
afraid. He got through a fortune of fifty thousand pounds in three years and
now he's in Queer Street.
Laura But he looks so fine.
Dorcas He does. Very fine.
Sir Austin Whoa up there! Whoa, whoa.
Dorcas But for all that, the tall grey that he rides so well is not his own. He
  has been lent it to try out for someone.
Zillah If you ax me they all look fine.
Dorcas They do. They are kingfishers among sparrows, are they not?
Sir Timothy Thank you, Matthew, thank you.
Matthew I hope she holds up, Sir Timothy. I advise a-taking it easy.
Sir Timothy I will. Landlord!
Matthew Your health, Sir Timothy.

The Landlord gives Matthew a drink

Sir Timothy I think Mrs Gascoine also wants your opinion.
Matthew Right you are, Sir Timothy.
Zillah My, but look at that Mrs Gascoine. Look at her clothes. Looks for all
the world like she'd been melted and poured into 'em, now don't she?
Laura The one with the floating veil?
Zillah That's her.
Dorcas A perfect madam. Just look at all those men round her.

Laughter from Mrs Gascoine. The Hunt moves round

And there. Those two. Walking up and down, and pretending to soothe the
horses. D'you see her? A pretty quiet little thing?
Zillah I see her fine handsome young feller.
Dorcas He's only a farmer from Northamptonshire.
Laura Who's she?
Dorcas She's Sir Timothy's cousin, Lavinia.
Zillah He's wasting his time then.
Dorcas He is. Here comes her mother.
Mother Lavinia, accompany me at once.
Dorcas It'll never do, my poor dears, with him not having a penny to bless
himself, as the saying goes.
Sir Timothy Thank you Landlord, thank you.
Landlord I hope you draws the first covert, sir.
Sir Timothy So do we all, eh? What? Warm ourselves up a bit, eh?
Huntsman, you can whip them in.

Loony Joe makes noises

The Huntsman blows his horn

Sir Timothy Tally ho! Tally ho!

*Music. The Hunt gallops away. When everything is silent again Loony Joe
is alone on the Green, Matthew and the smiths drift back into the smithy and
Dorcas, Laura and Zillah are in the empty post office*

Zillah Well, if there's one thing I relish it's a bit of excitement and a look at
somebody who's something! Beef stew and dumplings for dinner, Miss
Lane, I reckon the men need 'em this weather. Oh! I hope Mrs Macey
caught her train in time. Did she?
Dorcas I imagine she must have done, yes.
Zillah Good for her.

No more is forthcoming. Zillah has perforce to go. But when she shuts the

*door behind her she listens at the keyhole. Dorcas expects no less. She waits
for a second or two and then goes to the door and flings it open. Zillah stands
up in surprise and annoyance*

Zillah Oh!

Dorcas Ah! There you are, Zillah. As I say, I am sure that Mrs Macey did
catch her train, and I think that I shall shortly come to the kitchen myself
to clarify the calves' foot jelly.

Zillah Oh! (*She goes, muttering to herself*) It's a sin, and a shame, is the way
I'm not told nothing in this house! Tells that hoity-toity Miss Laura though
don't she? Oh ay! Of course she do!

Zillah goes

Dorcas (*smiling and turning back to Laura*) Hunt Morning is always the
quietest of the year over this counter. You can well look after the office, I
think.

Laura Yes.

Dorcas Were you asked on the delivery why Mrs Macey was absent?

Laura Yes.

Dorcas What did you say?

Laura Sickness.

Dorcas Good (*She goes to leave but Laura checks her*)

Laura Is he a gentleman's gentleman?

Dorcas What?

Laura Mrs Macey's husband.

Dorcas Oh. Oh, he may have been once. I believe that latterly he was a
bookmaker.

Laura Oh, I say. You don't mean he wrote do you?

Dorcas Wrote?

Laura Like Sir Walter Scott and Shakespeare.

Dorcas No, Laura. No. His kind of bookmaking had to do with betting on
horses.

Laura Oh.

Laura would ask more but Dorcas has her reason to go

Dorcas Well: I must look to the calves' foot jelly!

*In the forge hammers crash down on the anvil. One smith stands by the
bellows, two wield hammers, and Matthew holds the hot iron in tongs. Loony
Joe watches*

Solomon (*singing*) Oh, Bavour, will 'ee listen to what I have to say?
Bavour (*singing*) Speak now or forever hold they peace, I pray.
Solomon (*singing*) I just a-wanted to ask: does Loony Joe have any notion of why us is hammering away?
Bill (*singing*) You've axed him the same question these past six months, every day.
Bavour (*singing*) And the answer is still no a-cause Loony Joe's a decent cratur but soft in the upper storey.
Matthew Hold your tongues.

The post office doorbell rings and Cowman Jollife enters. He is an old man who lives with his wife in the large and otherwise deserted farmhouse on the same side of the Green as the post office

Jollife Morning, young missy.
Laura Morning, Mr Jollife.
Jollife Penny stamp, please.
Laura How's Mrs Jollife today?
Jollife Turned the corner, thank 'ee kindly.
Laura That's very good news.
Jollife Oh ay. Un's turned the corner. (*He has his stamp but does not move*) Er — I hear you a-took Mrs Macey's delivery.
Laura Yes.
Jollife Well, I been a cowman all my life, and in case you takes the delivery again, I'll tell 'ee what I told Mrs Macey when 'er first come here. If you're crossin' a field and you wants cows to get out o' your way, let 'em see what you be up to. Let 'em see that you be in a hurry, and they'll make way for 'ee. They be knowin' old craturs, cows.
Laura Thank you.
Jollife (*still he does not move*) Er — no trouble over Mrs Macey, be there?
Laura Trouble? No. Sickness.
Jollife Well — I'll just pay my respects to Matthew afore I go.

More sledge-hammers in the forge. The smiths sing "The Holly and the Ivy". Then Matthew checks them

Matthew Right, lads. Over them coals again. Come on. Stop singing and give us room.
Bavour (*singing*) Oh Bill, you mun blow them bellows!
Matthew (*can't help singing himself*) I said stop singing and — (*He checks himself and speaks normally*) I said stop singing and give us room.

Loony Joe is very interested

Solomon Give us room, Joe. Give us room.
Jollife (*entering the forge*) Morning, boys. Morning, Matthew.
Matthew Morning, John.
Bill Morning, Mr Jollife.
Jollife What's that?
Matthew What do her look like?
Jollife Her looks to me like a big drain flap.
Matthew Ay. Her's a big drain flap.

Loony Joe makes noises

Bill (*mimicking Loony Joe*) Great big drain flap.
Jollife They say it's sickness what kept Mrs Macey from taking her delivery.
Matthew Ay.
Jollife In that case, why were Doctor Henderson seen a-driving her and her son Tommy in his gig to Candleford railway station?
Matthew No use asking us. We've been working hard all morning, ain't we boys?
Bavour Ay.
Matthew Talking of sickness, though, how's Mrs Jollife today?
Jollife Un's turned the corner, Matthew, thank'ee kindly.
Matthew I'm pleased to hear it.
Jollife By hem, but she were as sick as a dog last week. I sat up with her six nights running. Never had my clothes off.
Bill You didn't flinch though, eh, Mr Jollife?
Jollife I did not. I pulled her through, for she didn't flinch neither.

They take the drain flap back to the anvil for a last shaping hammer

Matthew Ay. It's a good long while I've knowed you and Mrs Jollife, ain't it, John?
Jollife It is. A good long while.
Matthew Afore Miss Lane were born. Her father were in charge here, weren't he?
Jollife He was.

They smile at the remembrance. Loony Joe watches them and makes his joining-in noises

Ay, and that's afore you were born, Joe. It is. Poor Joe, eh? Loony Joe.

Loony Joe grins

I remember the day when his father — I brought my cows in from

Blackwell's Field and there was his father in the yard. Didn't know where to put hisself for the shame of it. They'd just a-found out young Joe here was a loony, see?

The men hammer. Then they stop

Ay. "John," says his father to me, "the cratur's no sense, and where there's no sense there's no feeling. But I know there *be* feeling," he says to me, "I know the cratur has feelings same as us do, for I've looked into his eyes and seen 'em full of tears."

Silence. Joe grins. He is pleased to be the centre of attention

Matthew He were a good man, were Joe's father.
Jollife His mother's a good 'ooman.
Bill Well, she's the one person he understands, ain't she, talking to him in signs like that.
Bavour He don't half go at turning that mangle for her.
Jollife What I says is, that it's all very well now with her takin' folks washing but what happens when her passes on?
Solomon Well, I don't reckon he'll take to the woods and hedgerows.
Jollife He might. Left to hisself he might.
Bill He can't shave nor nothing. His mother does it for him.
Bavour How long would it be afore his beard reached his knees?
Matthew That's enough. He'll not take to the woods, for if there's one thing he won't be, it's left to hisself.
Jollife He won't. He'll be put in the workhouse; or worse.

Silence. Loony Joe watches their sombre faces. Then he puts his arm round Jollife to comfort him. Then he is shy and withdraws it and stands aside like a little boy

Matthew You come back in, Joe. You come back in and warm yourself.

Slowly Matthew's smile and open hand coax Loony Joe into the group again

Jollife I'll tell 'ee what, Matthew.
Matthew What?
Jollife That poor cratur makes my heart sink, and allus has done.

Silence

Matthew (*deciding the mood has become too serious*) Come on. Let's finish this work afore dinner.

They heat and hammer the next drain flap. Loony Joe watches quietly. Then suddenly he bursts into loud inarticulate cries. Then he turns and runs quickly out into the snow

By hem! What were that about?

Solomon Don't know, do we — nor never will.

Bavour Ask me, old Loony Joe's like the monkeys. Monkeys could talk if they'd a mind to, but they think if they did we'd set 'em to work.

Laughter

Matthew Come on, you monkeys — back to work.

Jollife So ... er ... You can't tell me nothing about Mrs Macey, then?

Matthew We've been workin', John. No time to spit out nor nothing.

Joliffe feels a bit thwarted but puts a good face on it. He decides to go

Jollife Ay, well! Time for my own taties, eh? Poor Loony Joe, eh? Poor Loony Joe.

Jollife goes and as he does so the band plays "Poor Loony Joe"

Song

Band
Poor Loony Joe
What does he know
Where will he go
Poor Loony Joe

Poor Loony Joe
Where can he go
Out in the snow
Poor Loony Joe

Poor Loony Joe
They will shut you in
In the madhouse yard
Poor Loony Joe

In the fields Loony Joe is delighted to see the entire Hunt gallop past him, horns blowing, music crashing

Sir Timothy Tally ho! A gallop a gallop!

Sir Timothy's horse stumbles. Sir Austin reins up. They are alone

    Oh dash and blast it! She's gone lame!
Sir Austin What?
Sir Timothy Lame.
Sir Austin Oh, no!
Sir Timothy She jolly well has.
Sir Austin I don't think I should stop, old boy.
Sir Timothy Absolutely not, Austin. You press on.
Sir Austin Sorry.
Sir Timothy Don't talk rot.
Sir Austin I will press on, then.
Sir Timothy Every man for himself, Austin.
Sir Austin I know. I mean, suppose Mrs Gascoine needs assistance? Tally
    ho! Tally ho! (*He gallops away*)
Sir Timothy Mrs Gascoine? Good grief! The fellow's an incorrigible rake.

*In the living-room at Candleford Green it is the dinner hour. Dorcas is at the
head of the big table, carving. Zillah bustles in with the dumplings*

Zillah Shall I call Miss Hoity Toity from the post office?
Dorcas We each have our own clocks, Zillah: and I do not find Miss Laura
    hoity toity.
Zillah She still walks her wet feet across my clean floors.
Laura (*entering*) My, but those dumplings look good, Zillah.
Zillah Huh!

*The seating at table is ritualistic. Dorcas sits at the head. At her right hand
is Matthew and then Laura. Then there is a gap and then the three smiths sit
three abreast on the end of the table, facing Dorcas. Zillah sits at a small table
of her own at one side. The men have especially thick plates and drink out of
horns and not glasses*

Zillah Shall I call the men?

No response

    I call it shameful to keep good meat a-waiting.
Dorcas I hear them at the pump, Zillah.

The pump water is bitterly cold

Bill Oh, 'un's freezing!

Solomon Ah!
Bavour Oh!
Dorcas (*not appreciating their noise*) Really: if there weren't three wells on the property we might not have running water at all in frosts like this.

The men arrive with horse-play outside the door

Bavour (*singing*) I'll come up behind you with very cold hands!
Solomon Ah!
Matthew Sssh! ...

Matthew and the men tiptoe into the room. Their entire demeanour changes. The smiths do not speak until spoken to, and then only in low hoarse voices. Matthew is respectful but very much the senior man. They all sit and plates and food are passed in silence. The men do not eat but wait for Dorcas, the last served, to take her first mouthful. Then they all set to. Eventually Dorcas speaks

Dorcas William.
Bill Er — me, madam?
Dorcas You. I heard you shouting at the pump.
Bill Beg pardon, ma'am.
Dorcas I hope you do, for you seem to do more shouting than work nowadays.
Bill Ma'am?
Dorcas I understand from Farmer Stimson that one day last week when his daughter walked past the Smithy you came to the door and shouted "Whoa, Emma!" Is this true?
Bill Yes, ma'am.
Dorcas What have you to say about it?
Bill Beg your pardon, ma'am.
Dorcas Is that all?

A dreadful silence from Bill

You don't really think that young ladies are horses, do you?
Bill No, ma'am.
Dorcas Then why say "Whoa!" to one of them?

Bavour and Solomon catch each other's eye and giggle

What did you say?
Bavour Er — I was just asking Solomon to help me to the salt, ma'am.

Zillah Help you to salt, help you to sorrow, ain't that what they say?

Dorcas Never mind what they say, Zillah. I'd expected more of you, William. I'd expected civility at least.

Matthew I'll keep my eye on him, Miss Lane.

Dorcas I think you should, Matthew. Thank you.

Zillah My old mother knew a body who was helped to salt and what happened?

Matthew Eh?

Zillah I'll tell 'ee what happened. The gypsies stole her child away. That's what happened.

Dorcas In my opinion people's fear of gypsies is ridiculous. I mean, why should gypsies want to steal anybody? Surely to goodness they've got enough children of their own.

Zillah Some have supped sorrow with a spoon. That's all I'm a-saying. Some have supped sorrow with a spoon.

Everyone eats in silence

Laura Mr Jollife was in the office, Miss Lane.

Dorcas Indeed?

Matthew He passed the time o'day with us and all.

Laura He said that Mrs Jollife was improved. She's turned the corner, he said.

Dorcas I'm delighted to hear it. We must roast her a chicken and send it round for her supper tonight. Can I leave that to you, Zillah?

Zillah You can. I'll kill 'un first thing after this.

They all eat in silence

Dorcas I trust the hunt went well, Matthew? Did you keep a note of all the work we did?

Matthew Ay. I did. If you ask me, Miss Lane, Sir Timothy's like to drive that mare of his lame, but o' course I can't say don't take her out. And that new grey of Sir Austin's were as near as dammit — beg pardon, ma'am — it were very near to nippin' my ear.

Giggles from the smiths. Dorcas looks sharply at them

Solomon Ask me, ma'am, a groom oughter stand by and hold the young devil.

Matthew That he ought. Oh — and early on we had old Whitefoot in to be rough shod.

Zillah Poor old Whitefoot, eh? Poor old boy.

Bavour Ask me it's about time he was pensioned off — a-beggin' your pardon, ma'am.

Bill He went to sleep, ma'am. Nearly fell down on top of us.

Dorcas Let's see, Matthew. How old is Whitefoot now, do you reckon?

Matthew Twenty if he's a day. Well — Miss Elliot's father used to ride him to hounds, and he's been dead these ten years.

Zillah Poor old horse, eh?

Matthew You leave old Whitefoot alone. He'll drag that cart for another ten years, for what's he got to pull? Only young Jim and he's a seven-stunner, if that, and maybe a bit o' fish and a parcel or two. No, you take my word for it, old Whitefoot ain't going to die while he can see anybody else alive.

They hear the bell on the post office door

Laura I'll go.

The customer is the Vicar, Mr Coulsdon, old, rich, white-haired and benign

Good-day, Mr Coulsdon.

Coulsdon It's more of a galoshes day if you ask me, Laura. I was just passing and I thought I'd drop in to remind the journeymen of the special choir practice tonight.

Laura Ah!

Coulsdon I daresay it's not strictly necessary but it is the Archdeacon's sermon tomorrow and I do like the voices to be in fine old fettle for him.

Laura Er ...

Coulsdon They've not forgotten have they?

Laura No. Er — it's the men's bath night Wednesdays and Saturdays, Mr Coulsdon.

Coulsdon You mean they may be a little late?

Laura Yes.

Coulsdon But scrubbed at least.

Laura Yes.

Coulsdon Probably more than can be said for some! My greetings to Miss Lane!

Mr Coulsdon goes and Laura returns to the living-room

Laura It was Mr Coulsdon. He asks you to remind the men about the special choir practice tonight.

Bill (*groaning*) Oh ... !

Dorcas Did I hear a groan?

Bill Just me a-moving my chair, ma'am.

Dorcas Did you say tonight was a bath night?
Laura Yes.
Dorcas So Mr Coulsdon knows that our contingent will be late?
Laura Yes.
Dorcas Good.
Zillah What I says about Mr Coulsdon is that he's a gentleman who *is* a gentleman, and his lady's a lady. He never interferes with no-one's business and he's good to the poor.
Dorcas He is. He has extensive private means and he puts them to good use.

Silence. The men have finished. They make signs at each other. Matthew nods and jerks his hand

Solomon Er — beg pardon ma'am.
Dorcas Certainly. You are excused.

The three smiths get up and go. Outside, Bill wipes his brow

Bill By hem, but my knees were knocking together!
Solomon Sssh!

Mr Wilkins the carrier arrives

Journeymen Afternoon, Mr Wilkins.
Wilkins Afternoon, lads.
Dorcas I fancy I heard the carrier's cart.

Laura gets up again to go to the post office. Wilkins enters the post office

Laura Good-afternoon, Mr Wilkins.
Wilkins Good-afternoon, Laura. One parcel of clean clothes as per usual from your mother at Lark Rise. Have you got your dirty washing to go back?

Laura hands him a parcel

Thank you, and one copy of today's *Times* for Miss Lane, and a parcel to go.

Zillah enters with a mug of tea for Wilkins

Zillah Afternoon, Mr Wilkins.
Wilkins Afternoon, Zillah.
Laura How do you find this weather, Mr Wilkins?

Wilkins I find this weather and scenery the same: a bit dead, right away from the sea like this. Strange ain't it? Ship's carpenter for twenty years; visit my old uncle at Candleford, meets Mrs Wilkins as she now is and here I am with a horse and cart. Ay, this weather's cold, but more than that, 'tis dead. I've seen waves like the wall of a house coming down on your ship; and other seas, calm and bright as a looking-glass, with little islands and palm trees; but treacherous too. And treacherous little men in palm-leaf huts, their faces as brown as that, Laura. (*He indicates the counter*) And once I was — I suppose I did tell you that once I was shipwrecked?

Laura I can hear it told again, Mr Wilkins.

Wilkins Ay, oh ay. Well—I spent nine days in an open boat, the last of them without water. My tongue stuck to the roof of my mouth, like this. See? Stuck to the roof of my mouth. When I was rescued I spent ten weeks in hospital. All the same — all the same, I'd dearly love one more trip. But my dear wife would cry her eyes out if I mentioned it. And the business, of course, couldn't be left. There's my old horse for one thing. Couldn't take him in no Bristol tramp steamer, could I?

Laura Well, perhaps he could work the donkey engine.

Wilkins Donkey engine? Ha ha. That's a good 'un.

Laura pays for the parcel

No, I've swallowed the anchor, all right, I've swallowed the anchor.

Mr Wilkins goes

The band sings "Haul away the anchor"

Song

Band   And it's time to go now,
Haul away the anchor
Haul away the anchor
'Tis our sailing time,

With the breeze to guide us
Haul away the halliard
Haul away the halliard
'Tis our sailing time.

When my body's drownded
Haul away for heaven
Haul away for heaven
God be by my side.

Zillah takes the dirty dishes out of the living-room. Laura enters and hands
Dorcas The Times

Dorcas Thank you, Laura.
Laura Miss Lane, suppose Mrs Macey don't come back tonight?
Dorcas She will.

Silence

If she doesn't, you must take her delivery again.

Silence

If people ask where she is, you should say that ... (*She checks herself. She*
puts down the paper. She is too honest a woman to deceive Laura for long)
I take the meaning of your silence, Laura. If there is a truth to be withheld
you *should* know what it is; and Mrs Macey did say that I might trust you
as I thought fit. As you know, Mrs Macey was born near here. Her father
was a farm bailiff. Then the family moved, and for fifteen years she lived,
and was herself married, in London. Five years ago she returned to the
Green with young Tommy and I was able to obtain for her the post of Letter
Carrier. She had confided in me that her husband was in prison.
Laura Oh.
Dorcas He's in Reading. He is dangerously ill with pneumonia. That is why
she was sent for.
Laura Oh.
Dorcas As I say, I knew that the man was in prison, but not until today what
crime had caused him to be there.

Zillah sweeps in. She takes out the rest of the plates, etc. All in silence. Zillah
goes

Dorcas sighs. Then she continues

I told you that Mrs Macey's husband was a bookmaker. In the course of it
he was involved in a public-house quarrel which led to blows, and from
blows to kicks, and a man was killed. The crime was brought home to
Macey and he was given a long sentence for manslaughter. As far as young
Tommy knows, his father is a gentleman's servant travelling abroad. Now
he must be told the truth and prepared for what might follow. Macey's
sentence expires in a year and if his conduct has been good he will be
released sooner, unless — well, unless he dies now through his illness,
which in my opinion is the best thing that could happen. Still a husband is
a husband, and often the worst husbands are the most mourned for. Not that

I know whether Mrs Macey will be relieved or sorry if the Lord see fit to take him. I've certainly never seen a poor creature more upset by bad news. My heart aches for her, having to make such a journey, and snow on the ground, and a prison hospital and all manner of humiliations at the end of it. Such is life. Will you have another jam tart, Laura?

Laura (*she does not want one*) If Mrs Macey does stay away, I'll say it's her mother who's ill and Mrs Macey's gone to London to nurse her.

Dorcas Good. So will I.

Dorcas reads her paper. Laura gets up and wanders to look at the books. Dorcas realizes what Laura is doing and looks up. Laura's hand has strayed near one of the books

Is that Lord Byron's *Don Juan*?

Laura No. It's Hume's *History of England*.

Dorcas Byron's *Don Juan* is a terrible book, and most unfit for you to read. I don't know why I haven't destroyed it long ago. Next time there's a bonfire in the garden I must see about it.

Laura withdraws her hand. Maybe the book was Don Juan

In my opinion it looks unbusinesslike when the public enter the post office for the clerk to be reading, even David Hume or Shakespeare. If there is time that can be passed by reading, are you sure that you can learn nothing more from the Rule Book?

Laura I think I know most of it by heart.

Dorcas Only most of it? I must test you.

The post office doorbell rings

Laura I'll attend to it.

The telegraph machine starts up

Dorcas Good heavens! Not even our rush hour and everything happens at once!

While Dorcas takes down the telegraph Laura goes to the post office. Minnie, the telegraph girl stands there. She is fifteen, slow, languid, lost in her dream of herself as a person of beauty and finery. At the moment however she has a heavy cold

Laura Minnie! Are you better? We were all worried about you.

Minnie I've still got this dreadful cold, Laura. Has there been many telegrams?

Laura One or two this morning, I think, and one just came in.

Minnie Who delivered 'em?

Laura I think Mrs Gubbins took them, on her way home.

Minnie I've been sick as a dog.

Laura Have you?

Minnie I've felt all fainty, like.

Laura Oh dear.

Minnie I'd not have known where to lay my head but for what I overheard Mrs Green say about me last week.

Laura Oh.

Minnie Course, I told you then, didn't I?

Laura No.

Minnie She thought I didn't hear but I did.

Laura What did she say?

Minnie She said: that Minnie Hickman, she said, that Minnie Hickman 'ud manage to look well-dressed if she went around wearing a dishcloth.

Laura Very nice.

Minnie Think it's true, do you?

Laura Well ...

Minnie I do, although I says it myself. I look at my reflection in ponds when I'm out taking a telegram.

Dorcas (*sweeping in*) Ah. Minnie. You've come back just in time. There's a telegram for Mrs Herring.

Minnie Oh, I can't deliver no telegrams.

Dorcas What?

Minnie I've still got this dreadful cold.

Dorcas You've just walked across the Green.

Minnie I know, I felt real fainty. I said to Mum, I said, I must go and tell 'em I still can't deliver no telegrams.

Dorcas Minnie: Mrs Herring lives next door to your mother.

Minnie Of course she do.

Dorcas Then you can take her telegram as you go home, can't you?

Minnie D'you think I should?

Dorcas Yes. I do. And I think that whenever you feel fainty in future you should put your head firmly between your knees.

Dorcas gives Minnie the telegram. Minnie can't think of anything to do except go and take the telegram with her. Dorcas sighs at her departure

That girl is at that awkward age, neither woman nor child, when they should be shut up in a box for a year or two.

On the Green the footmen, John and Robert, meet Minnie

John Wert up! It's that there Minnie Hickman.

They pelt Minnie with snowballs

Minnie Oh!
Robert Whoa up, Minnie.
Minnie Oh! Don't you dare do that again, d'you hear!
Robert Only a bit o' fun, Minnie.
John Nothing to stop you throwing one back, Minnie.
Minnie Oh yes there is.
John What?
Minnie This telegram I'm a-delivering, that's what!
John Oh, get you off.

They pelt Minnie who runs away. Solomon sees them and comes out of the forge

Solomon Come on, lads! It's them rascals from the hall.

There is a brisk exchange of snowballs, stopped by Matthew

Matthew Get back, young Solomon. My word and haven't young folk today got a nerve.

The footmen walk up the space to the post office. Matthew throws a snowball after them

Robert Right. Come on then. Post office.

Robert leads the way. At the threshold John stuffs a snowball down Robert's neck. Robert blunders into the office and stands in a state of discomfort

   Aaargh!

Dorcas and Laura look up

Dorcas Well, don't stand there like a statue. What d'you want?
John Letters, ma'am. To be called for at the post office.
Dorcas Name?
John Gaskin.

Dorcas looks sharply at Robert

Robert Bowler.
Laura I'll get them.
John Thank you.
Dorcas Was it a hard walk from the Hall?
John Not too bad in the lanes.
Robert I thought it were easy until — (*Melting snow runs down his back*)
Aaargh!
Dorcas Are you in pain?
Robert No, ma'am.
Dorcas Then what's the matter?
Robert Stiff neck, ma'am.

Laura gives John the letters

John Did you ask about bringing these letters?
Laura No.
John I didn't reckon you would.
Laura I've not had time.
Dorcas What? What's that?
John Just remarking on the time, ma'am. Thank you , ma'am.
Robert Thank you.

They go, Robert still feeling uncomfortable

John "I haven't had time". Too proud to wear pattens, she is.
Robert See all this snow on the green?
John Eh?
Robert I'm a-going to rub your face in it!

*There is a chase suddenly brought up short as they confront Sir Timothy who
is on foot*

Sir Timothy Gaskin? What's this?
John Afternoon, Sir Timothy.
Sir Timothy Men in my livery don't behave like lunatics.
John Sorry, sir.
Robert Just collecting our letters, sir.
Sir Timothy Bookmakers' circulars again? Betting tips?

John and Robert are silent

Well. When you get back you can say that I'll be home early. The mare
went lame.
John Yes, sir.

Robert Right, sir. Thank you, sir.
Sir Timothy Matthew. Are you there, Matthew? She's gone wrong again. I'll have to walk her home.
John I tell you what.
Robert What?
John If that stuck-up gal's to take over Mrs Macey's delivery I'll pull her hair for her!

Robert and John go

Sir Timothy enters the post office

Sir Timothy Ha! Ha! Here is our future Postmistress General. What is the charge for a telegram of thirty-three words to Timbuctoo? Ah! I thought so. You don't know without looking it up in a book, so I'll send one to Oxford instead and hope you'll be better informed next time I ask you. There! Can you read my handwriting? I'm dashed if I can always read it myself. Well, well. Your eyes are young. Let's hope they'll never be dimmed with crying, eh, Miss Lane?
Dorcas Let us hope not.
Sir Timothy And I see you are looking as young and handsome as ever yourself. Do you remember that afternoon I caught you picking cowslips in Godstone Spinney? Trespassing, you were, trespassing; and I very properly fined you on the spot, although I was not as yet a JP—not by many a year. I let you off lightly that time although you made such a fuss about it.
Dorcas Oh, Sir Timothy, how you do rake up things! And I wasn't trespassing, as you very well know; it was a footpath your father ought never to have closed.
Sir Timothy But the game birds, woman, the game birds ...! Once gone can't be mended. Remember the elm trees that fell in the autumn gales? Wouldn't have lost them for worlds! Known them all my life. Opened my eyes on them, in fact, for I was born in the room they faced. Wouldn't have lost them for worlds. How much is that?
Laura Three and sixpence, Sir Timothy.
Dorcas Laura made the Hall delivery today.
Sir Timothy Really? Gave you a cup of tea, did they?

Laura smiles

I see the footmen had their mail sent here. That's not happened in a while. Didn't try to persuade you to carry it up there, did they? What?
Laura No.
Sir Timothy Because if they did I'll have them know I'm a JP.

Laura They didn't.

Sir Timothy Good. Well, Miss Lane: the Archdeacon's sermon tomorrow. Let's hope that it's shorter than the last one.

Dorcas I'm not sure that I heard what you said then, Sir Timothy.

Sir Timothy Ever the soul of tact, Miss Lane. Extra choir practice. Solemn occasion. I don't think that really I would miss it for the world. Good-day!

Sir Timothy goes

Dorcas Good-day, Sir Timothy. (*To Laura*) Did you have trouble with Sir Timothy's footmen?

Laura No.

Dorcas Are you sure?

Laura Yes.

Dorcas Do you sympathize with them?

Laura Yes.

Dorcas The older we get the more problems we discover, don't we?

Laura Yes.

Dorcas Such is life.

Dorcas returns to the living-room

Ben Trollope and Tom Ashley cross the green. They are old army pensioners. Ben is a tall, upright old fellow with a neat, well-brushed appearance and clear straight gaze. Tom is more retiring, a little shrunken, bent and wizened

Ben Pick your feet up, soldier. Pick 'em up.

Tom I'm freezin' cold.

Ben I know you're a-freezing, Tom. I know it.

They enter the post office

Ben Afternoon, missy.

Laura Afternoon, Mr Trollope. Didn't expect to see you in this snow, Mr Ashley.

Tom Didn't expect to see myself.

Laura When were you here last?

Tom Three months ago.

Ben Last time us pensions were due.

They present their books. Laura checks them. There is money in the counter drawer

Them's due again today and I said today's the day we should collect 'em!

Tom I said, "Look here, I've got my mending and cooking to do", but being the Sergeant he says, "Quick march".

Laura How's your garden in all this?

Ben Geraniums and fuschias is indoors; t'others takes their chance. Interested in flowers, aren't you, missy?

Laura Oh, yes.

Ben Ay.

Laura I like the way you line yours up, like soldiers.

Tom That's what we was, missy!

Ben Seeing as you like flowers you'd be head over heels with India, wouldn't she, Tom, especially the Himalayas.

Laura Oh, but I know! Northward of the great plains of India, and along the whole extent, towers the sublime mountain region of the Himalayas, ascending gradually until it terminates in a long range of summits wrapped in perpetual snow ...

Ben Have you learned that by heart?

Laura From a book at school.

Ben Well, then, you deserve to go there yourself, for I never saw anything like it, never in my life! Great sheets of scarlet as close-packed as they grasses on the Green, and primulas and lilies and things such as you only see here in a hothouse, and rising right out of 'cm, great mountains all covered in snow. Ah! 'Twas a sight — a sight! And what scents, eh? What scents and smells! That's why we rented our cottage — 'cause it had jessamine over the door.

Tom Ay. The scent of jessamine.

Ben India, missy, India. I wake up sometimes and think I've heard the bugle. I think I'll smell all the smells and blink my eyes in the glare and see the mutineers come at us. Horsemen in the dust.

Tom Sergeant. I want my mother, Sergeant.

Ben Too late, son. Face your front and fire on the young gentleman's command.

Silence. Laura watches them

Ay. Ay. It seems to get hold of you, like, somehow.

Laura gives them their pension money

Thank you, missy. Good-day.

Music starts, very quietly, as they go. Outside they check

Tom Imagine it: forty year ago a wench jilted me so I took the Queen's shilling. I'd not be that downcast now.

Ben Haven't you left that curry on the hob?
Tom Ay; and I wish we were back in India, with a bit o' hot sun.
Ben T'ain't no good wishing, Tom. We've had our day and that day's over.
We shan't see India no more.

Ben and Tom sing their "Old Soldier's Song"

Song

Ben   I left my native country
                           I left my native home
                           To wear a soldier's tunic
                           And preserve the good Queen's throne.
                           I travelled out to India, the mutiny to quell.
                           I have visited sweet paradise, and seen the gates of hell.

Chorus   When we wore the scarlet and the blue,
Ben ⎫   We took the old Queen's shilling
Tom ⎭   When the Empire days were new.
                           Forward into battle, don't you hear the bugle call.
                           Raise the tattered standard and let me like a soldier fall.

Tom   I've seen the Himalayas and I've been to Katmandu,
                           Seen sights to dazzle Solomon,
                           The tales I could tell you.
                           From Banbury to Bombay,
                           All the good times have gone by,
                           Now don't believe the man who says, "old soldiers never
                               die".

Chorus   When we wore the scarlet and the blue,
Ben ⎫   We took the old Queen's shilling
Tom ⎭   When the Empire days were new.
                           Forward into battle, don't you hear the bugle call.
                           Raise the tattered standard and let me like a soldier fall.

They march off, as smartly as they can manage

Mrs Gubbins crosses the Green

Bill, Solomon and Bavour are passing in and out of the forge

Bill Whoa-up, lads!
Bavour Afternoon, Mrs Gubbins.

Mrs Gubbins Huh!
Solomon (*singing*) And huh say all of us!
        For she's a grumpy old sow like
        For she's a grumpy old sow like.
Mrs Gubbins (*arriving at the post office*) No sign of the post yet?
Laura No.
Mrs Gubbins Huh! Any news?
Laura News?
Mrs Gubbins You know.
Laura I don't.
Mrs Gubbins Mrs Macey.
Laura Oh ... !
Mrs Gubbins If there is, tell us now afore Brown comes.
Laura No. I mean there isn't. I mean, so far as I know there's been no word.
  Wait a minute — here he is now.

Postman Brown crosses the Green

Brown "Deep and wide ..."
Smiths Praise the Lord. Jesus saves. Hallelujah.

Brown waves cheerily to the smiths and enters the post office

Brown Afternoon, young Laura.
Laura Afternoon, Mr Brown.
Brown Mrs Gubbins.
Mrs Gubbins Huh!
Brown How was your delivery?
Laura Fine.
Brown I knew you'd not flinch.

Brown empties the postbag and they set to work

  Tell you what.
Laura What?
Brown As I was a-comin' up the Fordlow Lane, I see'd that there's them old
  gippos again.
Mrs Gubbins Gippos?
Brown Ay. Caravans and all!
Mrs Gubbins Time they was routed out o' them places, the 'ole stinkin' lot
  of 'em. If a poor man so much as looks at a rabbit he soon finds hisself in
  quod but their pot's never empty.
Brown There's a lot of people says they eats hedgehogs! Hedgehogs! He!
He!

Mrs Gubbins Hedgehogs! Ha! ha! ha!

Brown Hedgehogs wi' soft prickles!

Mrs Gubbins (*abruptly stops laughing*) I seed that Mary Merton on the Green.

Brown Eh?

Mrs Gubbins There's summat there as is not as it should be.

Brown Wind's changed an' all. Come round to the West. I could smell old Jollife's muckhill.

They work

(*Trying to keep his next remark sotto voce to Laura*) Any — er — any word from Mrs Macey?

Mrs Gubbins What? What's that 'un said?

Brown Nothing.

Mrs Gubbins Nothing?

Laura No.

Mrs Gubbins Huh!

They work

Mrs Gubbins (*holding up a letter*) Ha!

Brown Eh?

Mrs Gubbins Look us here, now! Miss Mary Merton. To be called for at the post office. Whose handwriting be that?

Laura I don't know.

Mrs Gubbins Certain are you?

Laura Yes.

Mrs Gubbins Huh!

They work

Brown Mrs Gubbins.

Mrs Gubbins Uh?

Brown How long have us knowed each other?

Mrs Gubbins Twenty-five year.

Brown Thirty.

Mrs Gubbins 'Appen thirty.

Brown Ay, and I'll be jiggered if you've ever spoke very much, except about other folk's business.

Mrs Gubbins You can tell that to Jesus.

Brown I have found Jesus, Mrs Gubbins, (*huge pause*) and if I mention you at all, I shall ask Him to help you, not tell tales about you.

Mrs Gubbins Did you or did you not ask young Laura if 'un had heard any word from Mrs Macey?

Brown opens his mouth to deny the charge and then realizes that he cannot. Mrs Gubbins chuckles

Brown I can't think what there is for you to laugh at.

Mrs Gubbins You. Rain, hail, sunshine or snow, you're the biggest ole gossip I've ever seed.

Brown I'm the — No, no. Not so. What it be is, that all sorts o' folks confides in me.

Mrs Gubbins Huh!

Brown Huh? Look 'ee 'ere. This very morning that Mrs Wardup what lives at the hungry end of the Green taps on her window when she sees me, and my word, but haven't she got worries what with her sister's son not able to stop himself bed-wetting.

Mrs Gubbins Bed-wetting?

Brown Ay.

Mrs Gubbins Fried mice.

Brown Fried mice?

Mrs Gubbins Fried mice for his supper stops a growed man a-wetting his bed, never mind a nipper.

Brown Fried mice. Well. I've never heard that one afore, have you, young Laura?

Mrs Gubbins Huh. (*She sighs and shakes her head at them. She's not surprised*)

They work

(*Finding another interesting letter*) Hallo. Here's one for that Co-lo-nel.

Laura Yes. Colonel Scott.

Mrs Gubbins Co-lo-nel.

Laura Colonel.

Mrs Gubbins Co-lo-nel.

Laura Colonel.

Mrs Gubbins Co-lo-nel as plain as the nose on your face. I don't know what they teach 'em at school these days.

They work

Brown Mind you. I have heard of black slugs for warts.

Mrs Gubbins Slugs?

Brown Slugs. For warts. You bind 'em on for a day and a night.

Mrs Gubbins Dead or alive?
Brown The slug? Alive. I saw it done once, twenty year ago, by a young chap as sorted parcels at Candleford.

They work

Mind you: when he took the slug off it were dead.
Mrs Gubbins What about the wart?
Brown Well, no more'n a week after, the young chap's transfer came through. General Post Office, Oxford. I never seen him again.
Mrs Gubbins But did 'un, or did 'un not, charm the wart?
Brown Dunno, do I? He still had 'un when he left Candleford.

Mrs Gubbins sighs

Is this 'ere, all the village delivery?
Mrs Gubbins Ay.
Laura Yes.
Brown I'll be off with 'un then — and come back with the letter-box post. (*On his way out he checks*) You'll notice it's a-thawed a bit.
Mrs Gubbins Eh?
Brown I said you'll notice it's thawed a bit. Allus the same. I'm jiggered if it's not. Thaws, and just starts to freeze again afore the afternoon delivery. (*Singing*) "Yes, Jesus loves me ..."

As Brown passes the forge the men are finishing their work. They sing as they go into the living-room for their tea. It is almost dark again. Lamps are lit

The men's tea is a different occasion from the midday dinner. Dorcas is absent and Zillah presides. Everyone else occupies their dinner seats, but without Dorcas and Laura the occasion is more free and informal. The meal itself consists of stacks of bread and butter and a "relish" — a bowl of hard boiled eggs, or brawn, or a pork pie, or cold sausages

Bill By hem! Shoeing that donkey was hard work!
Bavour He-haw! He-haw!
Bill He was very stubborn.
Zillah Which was topmost? Man or beast?
Bill Eh?
Zillah Last time I saw young Bill a-shoein' a donkey, I'm danged if I could tell the difference between 'em! (*Laughter*) Did any of 'ee hear how the Hunt went off?
Matthew Sir Timothy said they drew one in Causey Spinney.

Solomon I thought they would.
Zillah Ay. Causey Spinney.
Matthew That were afore Sir Timothy dropped out, o' course.
Bavour I wonder if that Mrs Gascoigne drew one, eh, lads?

Splutter of laughter

Zillah What's that, he said?
Matthew Language, lads. Look to your language.
Zillah Just let him repeat what 'un said.
Bavour All I said was I wonder if that Mrs Gascoigne ...
Matthew (*clearing his throat very loudly and then trying to take over the conversation*) Ay. Ay. The Hunt. Well I gave Sir Timothy's mare a rub with one of them balms from my cupboard.
Bavour Just what Sir Austin used on Mrs Gascoigne.
Zillah What?
Matthew One of them balms from my cupboard.
Zillah I dunno how you find a use for some of them things.
Matthew Use? Use? Keep a thing seven years and you'll always find a use for it.
Bill Don't we know it, eh, lads?

More laughter

Zillah Now look here, you lads. You ain't a-going to make me blush at my age so you say what you're a sayin' straight out!
Bavour All I'm saying is that I did hear once from Matthew ——
Matthew Never. I like horses, not people.
Bavour From Matthew, last hay-home supper, when we'd all had an extra mug o'beer like, I did hear more'n a thing or two about that Mrs Gascoigne.
Matthew Take no notice of him.
Zillah Eh?
Matthew What?

Splutters of laughter from the smiths

Zillah I want to hear what you told him.
Matthew I never said — I — I think you lads 'as behaved summat shameful today.
Zillah Course they have. What did you tell him?
Matthew All I said was what I'd heard from the Vet.
Zillah He knows everything that Vet.

Matthew Mrs Gascoigne was a parson's daughter wi' no money at all until she meets this Major what's old enough to be her father, and when he died ...

Solomon There's some as says he exploded.

Matthew Well whatever happened to him, she were left with all his money and a lot o' men chasin' her.

Zillah See? See? The golden ball rolls to everybody's feet once in a lifetime. That's what my Uncle Jarvis used to say, and I've seen it myself over and over.

Bavour Golden ball?

Zillah I'll say one thing for 'un, though.

Matthew Who?

Zillah That Mrs Gascoigne. She'll look handsome in her coffin. Colour goes, and the hair turns grey, but the framework lasts.

Bill Ay. Oh ay. And two heads be better than one.

Solomon That's why fools get married.

Bavour Now Solomon. There's more ways of hanging a dog than by killing it.

Solomon Nor of choking it with a pound of fresh butter.

Zillah My heart and eyes! It's the heat o'your brains that lights that forge, ain't it?

Bill (*rapping on the table with his mug*) Another pint please, Landlady!

Cheers and laughter

Dorcas (*shouting from the post office*) Less noise there please!

At tea everything becomes very subdued

Zillah (*voice low*) Pass us your mug.

Bill (*whispering*) Eh?

Zillah Oh, pass us your mug, you young fool.

Solomon Whoa up!

Zillah Eh?

Solomon There's a gig outside. Well, we'll be off then.

Bill It's the Inspector, Matthew.

The gig has brought Mr Cochrane, the Post Office Inspector from Oxford. He is a well dressed public-school educated Civil Servant. He enters the post office

Cochrane Miss Lane. Good-afternoon.

Dorcas Mr Cochrane.

Cochrane Did you receive my telegram?

Dorcas I did. Laura, this is Mr Cochrane, the Post Office Inspector from Oxford.

Laura How do you do, sir.

Cochrane Are you Miss Timms?

Laura Yes, sir.

Cochrane Hm ...

Dorcas Will you take tea, Mr Cochrane?

Cochrane Later perhaps; I — I must confess a weakness for your scones and cream, Miss Lane.

Dorcas smiles

However, my business today is not with you but with Postman Brown.

Dorcas Ah.

Cochrane Is he on the premises?

Dorcas We expect him imminently: with the letter-box mail.

Cochrane Perhaps I should wait.

Dorcas Certainly.

Brown arrives singing

Brown "Oh, happy day, when Jesus washed my sins away."

Brown enters the post office. He checks when he sees Miss Lane and the Inspector

Er — Oh. Evening.

Dorcas This is Mr Cochrane, the Post Office Inspector.

Brown Er — Evening sir.

Dorcas This is Postman Brown.

Cochrane Thank you.

Dorcas Laura.

Dorcas and Laura stand discreetly to one side

Cochrane How far is it to your home, Brown?

Brown It's in Candleford, sir. Eight miles.

Cochrane Before you go I must ask you about this new Sunday evening collection. I hear you object to doing it.

Brown Yes, sir. I do object.

Cochrane On what grounds, may I ask? Your colleagues have agreed, and there is extra pay for it. It is your place, my man, to carry out the duties laid down for you by the Department and I advise you for your own good to withdraw your objections immediately.

Brown I can't sir.

Cochrane But why, man, why? What do you usually do on a Sunday evening? Got another job? Because, if so, I warn you that to undertake outside employment of any kind is against the regulations.

Brown My job on Sunday evenings, sir, is to worship my Creator, who himself laid down the law "Keep holy the Sabbath day", and I can't go against that, sir. (*He is trembling. He mops his brow with a large, red, white-spotted handkerchief*)

Cochrane Takes a lot out of you, I suppose, this worshipping business? Better attend to the work which brings you bread and butter. That's all for now. I'll report what you've said and you'll hear further about it.

Brown Yes, sir. Thank you, sir.

Cochrane goes outside

Cochrane (*to Dorcas*) A cantankerous man. I know his kind. Out to make trouble. But he will find that he will have to fit in the Sunday evening work with his psalm-singing.

Dorcas Good-afternoon, Mr Cochrane.

He goes

Dorcas returns to the post office. She and Brown stare at each other

Brown Phew! I were shaking like a leaf!

Dorcas He will make you conform.

Brown Miss Lane, are you a Christian?

Dorcas I do not see that whether I am or not is any business of yours, but, if you particularly want to know, I am a Christian in the sense that I live in a Christian country, and try to order my life according to Christian teaching. Dogma I leave to those better qualified than myself to expound, and I advise you to do the same.

Brown Ah: I see you've not found Christ yet.

Silence

Dorcas I will speak to the Postmaster at Candleford, and ask him to intercede for you.

The band plays "Dare to be a Daniel"

Song

Band   Dare to be a Daniel,
             Dare to stand alone,
             Dare to have a purpose true,
             Dare to make it known.

             Standing by a purpose true
             Heeding God's command,
             Honour then the faithful few
             All Hail! to Daniel's band.

At the end of the song Laura is alone in the post office. It is dark

Laura The post office closed to the public at eight and during the last hour
Laura was always in attendance: and on this particular Saturday some of
the men from the Green went to Sir Timothy's to give their Plough Play at
the Hunt Ball.

We see the Plough Play

Matthew   A room. A room. A room to let us in
             We are not of the ragged set
             But of the Royal King
             Stir up the fire and strike a light
             And see this gallant act tonight.
             If you can't believe these few words I say.
             Step in Tom Fool and clear the way.
Bavour   In come I who's never been yet
             With my big head and little wit.
             But I can dance and I can sing
             By your consent we will begin.
Bill   In comes old Jerry Jessum
             Oh my back I carry a besom
             In my hand a dripping pan
             Don't you think I'm a jolly old man
             If you don't I do.

             This man's not dead he's in a trance
             Rise up young Jack and have a dance.

Jack does the Broom Dance

All (*singing*)	We are not London actors
	That act upon the stage
	Wc're just the country plough lads
	That plough for little wage.
	We've done our best that best can do
	And best can do no more
	We wish you all good-night
	And another happy year.
Matthew	A piece o' pudden
	A piece o' brown
	If you don't give us something
All	We'll plough up your lawn.
Matthew	Penny for plough boys only once a year.

Sir Timothy and his guests at the Hunt Ball dance to "The Huntsman's Chorus". In the brewhouse we see Bill, Bavour and Solomon. Matthew has had his bath and is tying his tie. He wears his best suit for choir practice. Solomon has just got out of the bath and is in his shirt tails, Bavour is about to get into the bath and Bill is reading the paper while he waits

Are you not getting in the bath, young Bavour?

Bavour Too hot, ain't it? Waiting for some cold from the pump.

Zillah barges in with two buckets of cold water

Bill Shut that door.
Solomon Whoa up!
Matthew By hem!

Baviour jumps in the bath to avoid Zillah. It is fiercely hot

Bavour (*yelling and standing up*) Ah!

Zillah pours in the cold

Oh!

Zillah Never seen nothing like it for namby pambies in all my life.

Bavour You said you was a-leaving that bucket at the door.

Zillah I seed a baby's bottom afore. I seed more babies' bottoms than daisies in the field.

Bill Course you have. On account of how old you is.

Zillah What? What's that?

Matthew What he's trying to say is that the brewhouse on men's bath night ain't no place for a woman.

Zillah They should have stopped singing so they could hear my knocking.
Bavour It still ain't no place for a woman.
Zillah Oh. A woman now, am I? I thought I was an old beast of burden.

Bill and Solomon groan. Zillah opens the door and a draught blows in

Bill Ah!
Solomon Oh!
Zillah You might try giving a bit o' respect for a change, that's what you
    might try.
Bavour Shut that door!
Zillah Ha!

Zillah shuts the door and exits

Solomon Ay. There's a hemmed big draught with that door open.
Bavour Draught? I thought it was my happiness like to be nipped in the bud.
    I can tell you.
Solomon *(singing)* So go and leave me if you wish, love,
                Never let me cross your mind
                For if you think I am so unworthy
                Go and leave me, I don't mind.

Bill reads. Matthew is nearly ready. Solomon dresses

Bill Here we are. Here we are again.
Bavour What?
Bill Man knocked down by a bicycle.
Solomon Where's it a-going to end, eh?
Matthew Ask me, bicyclists oughter have roads to themselves, like railway
    trains.
Bill Course they ought.
Matthew Mind you, it's only a passing phase, when all's said and done.
Bavour What is?
Matthew Bicycling.
Bill You reckon?
Matthew Course I reckon.
Solomon So do I.
Bavour Says as much in the papers, don't it? So it must be true.
Matthew Ay. And what that means is: come what may, a good smith'll never
    want for a job.
Solomon Course he won't.
Bill Why not?

Matthew Because what ever may come of this new cast iron muck in other
ways, the horses'll always have to be shod, and they can't do that in a
foundry. Now, are you ready, young Solomon?
Solomon Ay.
Matthew Then let you and me get on and meet these two at the choir practice.
Bill Oh, not that door again.
Solomon Ready?
Bavour Ay.

The doors open

Ah!
Matthew What are things coming to, eh? When I was a young man I'd have
seen us stark naked under the outside pump and most grateful for it.

The door shuts and Solomon and Matthew exit

Bavour (*singing to tune of "British Grenadiers"*) Oh, Bill, pass us that towel
there 'cause I'm a-gettin' out.
Bill And about time to, if you was asking me.

*Bavour gets out. Bill is holding the towel. Zillah bursts in again. They leap
into the bath, using the towel to cover them both*

Bavour Ah!
Bill Oh!
Zillah You'm worse than girls. That's what you is.
Bill You've no right to be doing this.
Bavour Bursting in here like it was some corridor!
Zillah Forget my buckets, didn't I?
Bill I'll bucket you.
Zillah None of your lip, if you don't mind, young Bill. I've a-seen what
your're a-made of, and it ain't much.
Bill Don't you ...

Zillah opens the door to leave. The men gasp. She goes

Bill By hem!
Bavour Oh, come on. Hurry up. Tell you what.
Bill What?
Bavour We've got all the time us needs to think up a good April fool for that
Zillah.
Bill That we have.

Zillah (*entering*) I heard that. (*She throws two snowballs at them*)

Music. Laura and Dorcas have been sitting reading in the parlour. Mrs Macey crosses the Green and approaches the post office

Mrs Macey Hallo, anyone at home? Hallo?

Laura goes to let her in, followed by Dorcas

Laura Hallo. Is it you, Mrs Macey? Miss Lane, Miss Lane, it's Mrs Macey.
Dorcas My dear. Are you cold? Will you take some cordial?
Mrs Macey No. No, thank you. I left young Tommy in Reading. I have friends there.
Dorcas I know.
Mrs Macey What a day!
Dorcas Is — is your husband alive?
Mrs Macey Yes. He was over the crisis. He'll make a good recovery. He'll be released soon. I shall make a home for him. After all, a husband is a husband.
Dorcas Yes.
Mrs Macey Of course, I won't let him come here. Not to Candleford Green. Not to make a nine days wonder. I'll find rooms near my friends in Reading and the prisoner aid people can find him a job and if not — I can sew and I can — I shall be sorry to leave the cottage. I've had a few years' peace here. But we can't always do what we like or be what we want in this world can we? I must face the future, however much I dread it.
Dorcas Sit with us. Get warm.
Mrs Macey No, no, thank you. I left that old cat in the cottage, didn't I? I shall leave in a day or two. I'm sorry about the delivery. But a husband is a husband.

Mrs Macey leaves. Dorcas and Laura continue their conversation in the post office

Laura Miss Lane, why did you never marry?

Dorcas looks sharply

I'm sorry. Is that impertinent?
Dorcas My father came here as a journeyman smith. My mother was the master's daughter who fell in love with him. Her parents were outraged. They found her darning my father's socks and threw them on the fire. They said that after what they had done for her she must marry a farmer at least. But they relented. Mother and Father were married, and in time inherited

the house and the business. I was sent away to school. A weekly boarder. All the girls used to call each other "Miss So-and-so", even at playtime. When my father died he left me the business. Oh, everybody expected me to sell out and retire to Leamington Spa or Weston-Super-Mare but I carried on. Why not? I had kept the books and written the letters for many years, and Matthew is an excellent foreman. I suppose I took the post office because I like the notion of working to a time-table and being part of a national organization. I like people coming in and out and I like my scones and cream, too, and to read *The Origin of the Species* and bathe in warm rainwater and eau de cologne and to rub my hands and face with buttermilk and to follow in *The Times* the fluctuating fortunes of my shares. I suppose I sent for you because I see in you something of myself; a child I might have had. But, you know, I am only a tradesman's daughter. There are not many places in the world for women of our sort. We think too much. So there are not many husbands either.

Laura I'm sure I shall find a husband. I'm sure that he'll be tall and straight-backed.

Dorcas Like a knight imagined by Sir Walter Scott.

Silence

Sometimes, I don't see why you should ever leave here, Laura. You and I get on very well together, and perhaps after my time you might take my place in the office.

Laura walks out into the space which becomes the world of her memory and imagination and whole life. All the actors are there, in two lines

Laura It would have been pleasant to have lived all her days in comparative ease and security among the people she knew and understood. But she did not because she was eager and thought there would be more to life. There would be poems to write and a husband to love her and sons to cherish her and all manner of dreams to come true. Which one of them did, after a fashion, because her husband John was very straight-backed indeed.

John is there. Tall and narrow-minded and angry. It is the early 1900s, at night, in their miserable terraced house garden in Bournemouth. They have quarrelled and Laura has sought comfort in the snowy grass and trees

John All right. All right. What did I say then, eh? What did I say? All I said was that books is a waste of time and that as for your parading yourself as a writer of 'em, well, as my mother told you, think about me and our children. Think about us.

Silence

I have my ways and I stick to 'em, and so should you. I know it's hard with
children but that's your duty. I'm just home from work. I don't want no
arguments. Why did you run out here? Eh? Laura?

Laura I like the peace.

John You'll shame me out here.

Laura You say you're sorry.

John Not in my own garden, I won't. I have my ways and I ——

Laura Oh, jigger your ways.

John Cottage born, you are. Don't know the difference.

Laura I know better than you.

John No, you don't and you'll not look at me like that.

Laura Like what?

John You know.

Laura I don't.

John You know.

Laura I don't.

John Like I was nothing and you was clever.

Laura I love you.

John No, you don't.

Laura You're my husband.

John Prove it.

Laura Don't shout.

John Prove that I'm your husband. Kiss me. Show me you respect me.

Laura John.

John See, see? I don't want no arguments, nor never have. I have my ways,
it's you what's altered.

Silence

I don't know what to say. I wish you'd hold my hand.

Silence

Then suit yourself. Write your silly books.

Company (*singing*) At Jacob's Well a stranger sought
His drooping frame to cheer
His drooping frame to cheer.
Samara's daughter little thought
That Jacob's God was near
Samara's daughter little thought
That Jacob's God was near.

Laura When Laura was old and famous, John was proud of her books, but Laura was too lonely to care. The snows had dusted her with genius but she was too lonely to know. But in her cherished memories she saw always the children at Lark Rise, and Miss Lane, and the smiths as they beat the red hot metal into shoes.

Company (*singing*) This ancient well, no glass so true
      Britannia's image shows
      Now Jesus travels to Britain through
      But who the stranger knows?

      Yet Britain must the stranger know
      Or soon her loss deplore
      Behold the living waters flow,
      Come drink and thirst no more.

By this last verse the company have formed up into a photo pose. As the vocal ends the entire band takes up the tune and the Lights fade. They come up again. Snow falls. Slowly they disperse

Laura is alone. She walks across the space and the music changes. Company and audience perform the Grand Circle Dance

THE END

FURNITURE AND PROPERTY LIST

On stage: Cart
Snow and snowballs on Green

SMITHY:
Forge
Bellows
Tools
Anvil
Drain covers
Water pump

LIVING-ROOM:
Large table. *On it*: salt, pepper, remains of breakfast, cup of tea
7 chairs
Small table
Telegraph machine with telegrams under tea cosy
Books on shelves

POST OFFICE:
Bell over door
Counter. *On it*: mail, 3 postbags, private postbag, stamps, etc. *Under
it*: string, parcel. *In drawer*: money
Oilstove
Chair
Clock on wall

BREW HOUSE:
Bath
Newspaper
Chairs
Towels

Off stage: Practical storm lantern (**Laura**)
Practical oil lamp (**Zillah** and **Dorcas**)
Drinks (**Landlord**)

Set: IN LIVING-ROOM ON PAGE 88
Joint of meat, carving knife, knives, forks, plates, horns, plate of jam
tarts

Off stage: Dish of dumplings (**Zillah**)
                Parcel, copy of *The Times* (**Wilkins**)
                Mug of tea (**Zillah**)
                Postbag with mail, parcel (**Wilkins**)
                Mail (**Brown**)

Personal: **Hunstmen**: hunting horns
                Sir Timothy: note
                Tom: pension book
                Ben: pension book
                Brown: large red, white spotted handkerchief

Set: IN LIVING-ROOM ON PAGE 106
                Stacks of bread and butter, "relish", plates, cutlery, mugs, pot of tea

Off stage: 2 buckets of water (**Zillah**)

LIGHTING PLOT

Property fittings required: nil

Various interior and exterior settings

To open: House lights on

Cue 1	**Cinderella**: " ... we don't understand, Laura." *Fade house lights*	(Page 66)
Cue 2	After second verse *Bring up lighting on actors in pose*	(Page 66)
Cue 3	After second chorus *Change to pre-dawn lighting on* **Timms** *family*	(Page 66)
Cue 4	Music for Laura's journey ends *Change to first light on mid-winter morning*	(Page 68)
Cue 5	**Bill** lights the shavings. **Solomon** pumps *Forge fire flares and grows*	(Page 70)
Cue 6	**Laura** comes downstairs *Bring up dim lighting on living-room and post office*	(Page 70)
Cue 7	**Dorcas** and **Zillah** come into the living-room *Increase lighting in living-room with covering spot for oil lamp*	(Page 70)

Cue 8	**Laura** takes the lamp into the post office
	 *Increase lighting in post office with covering spot for
	   storm lantern; gradually increase lighting in areas
	   surrounding the house and smithy*
		(Page 70)

Cue 9	At the end of "Postman's Knock" *Increase lighting to winter daylight, cut practicals and covering spots*	(Page 79)
Cue 10	**Mrs Gubbins**: " ... any word from Mrs Macey?" *Begin to dim lighting gradually*	(Page 105)

Cue 11   Lamps are lit   (Page 106)
             Snap on covering spots for lamps in living-room and
                post office

Cue 12   **Matthew** (*singing*): " ... only once a year."   (Page 112)
             Bring up bright interior effect on Hunt Ball dance and
                dim interior effect on brew house

Cue 13   **Dorcas**: " ... take my place in the office."   (Page 116)
             Cross-fade to light on **Laura** *and actors in line*

Cue 14   The entire band takes up the tune   (Page 118)
             Fade to black-out. Bring up lighting on space with snow
                effect

EFFECTS PLOT

Cue 1   **Dorcas**: "Sssh! ... " They wait. Silence   (Page 80)
         Telegraph bell and machine

Cue 2   **Laura**: "I'll attend to it."   (Page 95)
         Telegraph machine